I0670799

Accept

the

Unexpected

Accept
the
Unexpected

by L. Cherelle

Resolute Publishing

Louisville, KY

ISBN-13: 978-0-9830948-0-7
ISBN-10: 0983094802
LCCN: 2010915512

First Printing

10 9 8 7 6 5 4 3 2 1

Cover Copyright © 2011 by Resolute Publishing, LLC. All rights reserved.
Cover Design /Layout by Lauren Curry
Acknowledgements: Zakiya Bediako, Casmen Jackson, and Chantelle Jones

Resolute Publishing, LLC
Louisville, KY 40201

www.respublishing.com
info@respublishing.com

*To my love and those I love,
know that anything is possible.*

February 10th

"DAMN," KELEYA WHISPERED as she stepped into her apartment. "Damn." Keleya shut and locked the apartment door and walked into the great room. She looked around shaking her head in disbelief. The dining room chairs lay horizontally. Coffee tables flipped. DVDs scattered. Curtains ripped. Picture frames busted. Plants uprooted. Pillows gutted. Lampshades stabbed. She figured Kris would take some stuff, but tearing up the apartment never crossed her mind.

Keleya walked around the room for a better survey of her belongings. She found the wooden West African mask that hung on the wall by the side of the chaise lounge split into two pieces. After staring at the mask infuriated, yet paralyzed by disbelief, she rushed to check the bedrooms. Untouched. And the bathrooms were too.

As she re–entered the great room a light caught her eye. She noticed the kitchen was intact with the exception of the refrigerator door that rest wide open. She walked to the refrigerator noticing all the sweating food. She shook her head and simply closed the refrigerator door before stepping into the pantry to grab plastic shopping bags for the glass shards and cotton mess.

ACCEPT THE UNEXPECTED

After everything was picked up, thrown away and back in place, I approached the mask again. Although broken and laden with splinters, it still meant everything to me as it did before. So I hung it up, centered above the sectional in two adjacent pieces. I knew that it looked strange, but I didn't care.

The day before

"YOU MUST THINK I'm some sort of fool," Keleya said nonchalantly with her right arm upright, fist supporting the weight of her head.

"What?" Kris asked.

"You know don't too much get pass me," Keleya continued. "I know you know that."

Kris sat silently on the far end of the sectional gazing at the flat screen, pretending to listen to an episode of Living Single while thinking, 'If she says *know* one more time.'

"Did you sleep with her?" Keleya asked with a little more emotion across her face.

"What!" Kris snapped.

"You fucking heard me!" Keleya fired back. "Did—you—fuck—her? And don't bullshit with me Kris!"

Kris looked at the TV again. Anytime Keleya began to excessively curse, she was legitimately mad. "What you gettin upset for?" Kris asked sternly. "You jumpin to conclusions."

"I ain't upset, but I will be if you keep stallin," Keleya said and exhaled. "Why the hell would you come back in here after you slept with her?"

Pushing all attempts aside to keep an argument at bay, Kris yelled, "Why you gotta jump to conclusions! That's yo problem. You think you know every damn thing. Shit! Just leave it alone!"

"Leave it alone? So I'm supposed to sit here and ignore the fact that you slept with that girl and tried to keep it shaded? If you think I'm gone do that, *you're* the fuckin fool!"

"So, *I'm* the fool now?"

"Yep," Keleya said with too much enunciation.

"First I'm a cheater. Now I'm a fool," Kris said sarcastically with raised eyebrows.

"You damn skip." Keleya stared at Kris. She was observing their relationship fall apart before her eyes and didn't know what to do or say next.

"Then why you here?" Kris asked after a moment. "Leave."

"Leave?" Keleya retorted. "Kris, I'm not one who just fucked up our relationship. I'm not the one who cheated and was foolish enough to keep a record of it through text messages! You—"

"So you going through my phone now?" Kris interrupted.

"You gave me a reason to *and* you gave the bitch a dedicated ring tone. I mean come on! Did you think I was not gone notice that shit?" Keleya asked, but there was silence. The look in Kris' brown eyes seemed to be an admission of guilt, so Keleya marked the moment. This was the moment that Kris might finally start to admit to infidelity. So damn the conclusions. This was all the confirmation Keleya needed. "I peeped that shit out when you started talkin *on* the phone," Keleya continued. "You don't do that. You *always* talk on the speakerphone up in here. And I really knew what was going on when your cousin came over here the other day smilin in my damn face, askin me how long I would be gone. Why the hell would Dréa ask me that? She ain't no more concerned with my work schedule than she is with the White lady across the street. Did you ask Dréa to ask me that? You just had to know that it would be your opportunity to get with her, huh?"

Keleya stared at Kris growing internally aggravated. She continued to think about the fact that the person she loved actually cheated. She couldn't stand the feeling of knowing she was just another Black woman who couldn't have a lasting, loving relationship. And knowing this made her feel defeated. She was also upset about reaching a state of emotional frenzy, breaking through the laid-back cloak that she usually bore. But instead of backing down and going into the bedroom to be alone, she decided to add fuel to the fire. "Y'all ain't made of muddy waters. Both of y'all transparent as hell. You must of thought I was stupid or some shit, and yo dumb ass, weed-head ass cousin thought I was too."

"Dumb ass?" Kris questioned. "Dumb! Keleya you got some mutha—!" The argument ensued and vehemently elevated. Keleya was now on her feet, allowing her defeat to be expressed through rage to the point where the verbal altercation was on the verge of becoming physical.

But Keleya abruptly stopped when she realized they had come to a threshold that had never been crossed before— violence. So she took the initiative to concede. She grabbed her purse and keys off the cherry dining room table and said with an unsettling coolness, "When I come back tomorrow you better have gotten your shit and you better be gone from *my* goddamn apartment." Neither Kris nor Keleya said another word. Keleya threw the purse over her shoulder with the ease of a woman who had done it a thousand times and proceeded to the door.

When I came back the next day, Kris was gone but the apartment was vandalized. And after I read the D—U—M—B—A—S—S that was etched in my coffee table, I knew that Dréa had come and left too.

February 11th

"WHY YOU SPEND the night at Momma house Tuesday?" Nkosazana asked.

Keleya didn't respond. She continued to walk beside her sister, listening to the sound of the wobbling wheel on the Walmart shopping cart as they walked down a frozen food aisle. Nkosazana stopped to get chicken fingers from the freezer. Not wanting to be rude with the silent treatment, Keleya replied, "Why don't you cook?"

Nkosazana ignored the evasive question and proceeded to pry information. "Momma told me you came over there round 11:30. She said you didn't say nothin. You just came in and went to sleep."

'Damn she tells you everything,' Keleya thought. "I don't wanna talk about it right now Zana."

"Right now? Leya ain't no later with you." Nkosazana stopped again to take six chicken potpies from another freezer. Once the door slammed, she continued. "You might as well tell me now. And don't turn around and say ain't nothin to tell you."

Keleya exhaled and scratched her scalp. She didn't have a problem talking about what happened the other night. She just had a problem talking about it with Nko–big mouth–sazana.

Tell her and the next thing you know Rita would call. Keleya didn't want her sister's growing grapevine to be watered with events in her life, so she prefaced her story with a warning. She looked her sister in the eyes and said, "Look...don't be tellin *nobody* what I'm bout to tell you."

"I won't," Nkosazana complied. Of course, Nkosazana didn't ease her sister's hesitation by saying, 'That's not my style. I don't tell other folks' business.' Instead, she says 'I won't' because she knew that she would.

"Me and Kris got into fight," Keleya shared.

"Whaaat?" Nkosazana said slowly like a seasoned gossiper.

"I don't mean like that. It was an argument. It could have come to that, but I left and went to Momma's house."

"What happened?" Nkosazana asked in a warm and concerned manner.

'You so fake,' Keleya thought. "Kris...slept with this girl we met—"

The shaky cart came to a halt. "What!" Nkosazana said sharply, so loudly that an older Black woman looked back to identify who shouted in the store. Keleya saw that Nkosazana was excited so she gave her sister a don't-play-with-me look. "How you find out?" she asked calmly, hiding her eagerness for the dirt that was to come.

"I just knew. Kris didn't come out and say it, but not sayin it confirmed it...plus Dréa let the cat out the bag too...and I had a feelin somethin was going on after we went out last Friday because—"

"Grab me a big box of Fruit Loops," Nkosazana interrupted.

"Are you listenin to me?"

"Of course," Nkosazana replied, but not too anxiously. She then looked puzzled so that Keleya would fill in the following question. "How you know for sure that Kris had sex with somebody else?"

"Because things have changed. Since..." Keleya paused to wait for another shopper to pass by. "Since we moved back to Memphis. And after we went to the club last week I could just feel it."

"Club?" Nkosazana asked comically. "*You* went to the club? Which one?"

"*The Lounge.*"

"The gay club on Madison?"

"Yeah. Dréa begged us to go so we went."

"How was it?"

"It was a'ight, but you know that ain't my scene."

"Is it nice?"

"Heeeell no." They both laughed. "Two more cracks and it would be a whole in the wall, and it was way too many folks up in there."

"Did any of them girls try to get at you?"

Keleya wasn't surprised that Nkosazana asked that question. Her sister claimed like every other Black woman that she was strictly dickly, but would smile hard as hell when a female showed some interest. Nkosazana, however, could never admit that flirtation is genderless. "There were some studs that looked bold enough, but no."

"So what happened?" Nkosazana asked in an attempt to speed up the story as they left the food center for women's clothing.

"Dréa was doing her Dréa thing. She—"

"I can't stand her ass," Nkosazana interrupted to add her two cents.

Keleya ignored the comment because Nkosazana had only met Dréa twice, briefly. "She knew almost everybody in there. You know they don't call her Dréa, they call her Drè. She can't be Dréa or Andréa out in public...they even give her free drinks. And when it came time for them to perform, she got on the stage and danced to *Bump N' Grind.*"

"Damn, she it took back didn't she?"

"Mmm hmm. She be into R. Kelly now. She got up there with her hat on, raising her shirt up to show off her abs while doing belly rolls and shit. Then she threw the hat in the crowd and brought some girl on the stage to sit in a chair. Then she bumped and grinded all over the girl and put her head all between the girl's legs."

"No she didn't," Nkosazana said, just as Black women do when the story is getting juicy.

"Trust me. That's nothin. I done seen and heard worse. But anyway, she made $47."

"What you mean she made $47?"

Before Keleya could answer the question, she had to stop her sister. "You don't need that shirt," she advised.

"Why not?" Nkosazana asked, holding a faux satin royal blue blouse.

"Yo stomach is too big for that," Keleya replied. Nkosazana rolled her eyes, placed the shirt back on the rack and walked to the next one. Keleya pushed the basket so that her sister could effortlessly sort through the garments. "I don't like that one either," she said next.

Nkosazana wanted to question her sister's objections, but she was well aware of her tainted dressing reputation within the family. Instead, she asked again, "How she make $47?"

"Folks in the audience gave her money."

"Like they do strippers?"

"Yeah."

"Hell, $47 for one song, I'd do it too...so where does the cheatin come into all of this," Nkosazana asked, no longer patient with her sister's slowly progressing timeline.

"There was this girl there that Dréa knew named Jazmine.

Dréa brought her over and introduced her. She was nice… cute…she started drinkin, got a lil loose and shit and start flirtin."

"Flirtin with who?"

"Everybody…at first, I didn't think nothin of it. But then I noticed the way that Kris looked at her. Kris was attracted to her, but it really didn't bother me cause there's always going to be somebody you find attractive, right?"

"Girl please! Do you think I'm gone watch my man drool all over another woman? Shiiit," Nkosazana said slowly.

"It wasn't like that. She wasn't there that long. She came and she left."

"So how did you know Kris took it there?"

"Intuition. Change in behavior. And I noticed a ring tone on some of Kris' texts. So I did what anybody would do. When Kris got in the shower on Tuesday, I went through the texts. And you know I ain't one to be pryin through nobody stuff."

"I know. That don't even sound like you."

Nkosazana's comment immediately made Keleya feel bad. She felt as if she'd let herself go because her actions were out of character. However, she pushed these feelings aside and continued. "Yeah…but I couldn't help it. Anyway, Kris had been carrying on a conversation with somebody new."

"What you mean somebody new?"

"Meaning in the conversation, the texts, they were gettin to know one another. Plus she said I had a good time, can't wait to see you again. And the texts were signed *Jazzi Girl*, so I knew who the hell it was. It was Jazmine."

"How you get Jasmine from Jazzi Girl?" Nkosazana questioned.

"It's obvious. J—A—Z—M—I—N—E is easily Jazzi."

"How you know that's how she spell her name?"

Frustrated with the questioning, Keleya said, "Look! It's her okay."

"Kris said it was?"

"No, but it is…anyway, Saturday I went to an event my job was having. It was the bowl all night fundraiser I was tellin you about that yo ass didn't show up to. I can't really remember if I told Kris I was going before that day, but I do remember sayin that I didn't know what time I'd be back. And Dréa was there when I left. I didn't get home til almost 2:00. Kris was gone, but I figured they went somewhere. And then Kris text me and said they were together."

"You mean with Dréa?"

"Yeah. But when I read the texts, I knew that was a lie."

Finally deciding there was no blouse to purchase, Nkosazana proceeded to health and beauty. After taking a quick phone call from her daughter, Janya, Nkosazana continued. "How you confront Kris?"

"I asked if Dréa was the one that hooked them up."

"So you just came out and asked?"

"Yeah, wasn't no need to be pretty with it. Anyway, it went downhill from there. We got into it and I left."

"Have ya'll talked?"

"No."

"Damn, that's messed up. But then again, you can't put nothin past nobody no matter how long ya'll been together."

"I guess not," Keleya sighed. "Hold up, let's go over here right quick. I need to get some pillows." Once at the destination, Keleya began to select throw pillows that matched her sectional.

"I thought you meant bed pillows. What you need those for?" Keleya didn't respond. She continued to look for three pair that she liked. "You need six?" Nkosazana questioned expressively.

"Yeah, I don't have any."

"What happened to the other ones?"

"Gone."

"And where do pillows go?"

"In the trash."

"Who throws away good pillows?"

"They weren't good anymore," Keleya said as she tossed her last selection in the basket. As they walked to the register, Keleya could feel her sister's burning stare. Nkosazana was impatiently waiting for an explanation about the pillow situation, so at checkout Keleya opened up. "I'm gettin the pillows cause Kris and Dréa ripped the other ones. When I left work and went back to the apartment, it—"

Nkosazana took hold of her sister's arm. "They fucked up your apartment?" Keleya pulled her arm back and shook her head yes. Nkosazana's jaw dropped. "How bad is it?"

"It was bad…but it was just the great room."

"Just!" Nkosazana yelled with offense. "Did you call the police?"

"No!"

"Why not? Just cause you been with Kris for four years don't mean they can tear shit up and not be accountable for what they did?"

"Look, I didn't and I'm leavin it alone. It is what it is and I…" Keleya paused upon noticing the cashier beckoning their attention. She motioned for her sister to begin placing items on the conveyor belt. "I'm done with this conversation."

It made me feel a little better to talk about the incident. But a few hours later, I regretted it because I realized how much I was actually hurt by everything Kris had done. I decided not to tell anyone else, not even JaCola. I hoped that Dréa and Nkosazana would be the only ones who knew what had occurred between Kris and me.

February 12th

KELEYA WOKE UP and started the day early. She went to Michael's to buy replacement letters for the bracelet her niece had broken. She had the day off from work, so she purchased a bag full of accessories to spend the afternoon making jewelry. When she got home, she immediately dove into her hobby, her stress reliever. She placed a movie in the DVD player and cleared the table for the blue bin of tools and parts. As she listened to *The Color Purple*, she remade Janya's bracelet while brainstorming designs for new pairs of earrings and matching necklaces. This was the ultimate therapeutic activity. Forty-five minutes into the session, her BlackBerry chimed. She leaned over to grab the phone. It was a text from Kris. Three days had passed since they last communicated.

> *I'm sorry about what happened. Can we meet/talk?*
> *Why?*
> *B/c I love you.*
> *Really?*
> *Yes or no?*

'Talk about what?' Keleya thought. 'Being together? Coming back here?' She sat there for three minutes trying to decide whether this was something she really wanted to do.

> *Ok. When? Where?*
> *2mrw, 1 pm at Rico's.*
> *No. 2 pm Sunday at Starbuck's down the street.*
> *K. I luv u.*

It's hard for me to resist Kris' affection. And Rico's is my favorite wing joint. I knew this was an attempt to get back in my good favor. The only thing I'm willing to give is my time, but Kris barely deserves that. So I didn't text back.

February 13th

AFTER EATING BREAKFAST, Keleya got dressed to go see her eldest sister, Stacy, and to give Janya the repaired bracelet. She didn't get much sleep the night before. She tossed and turned, constantly thinking about Kris and their upcoming meeting. But she went to her mother's house to spend the afternoon with her family anyway.

As Keleya walked through the carport, she could smell greens cooking. Her mother, Rita, was inside preparing an early dinner. Keleya smiled as she entered the house. She could hear sounds of her nieces and nephew laughing and playing in the den. Stacy was sitting at the kitchen table talking to Rita and eating homemade German chocolate cake. "Keleya I done told you bout walkin in this house without knockin first. You know I can't hear when you walk up in here. You gone mess around one day and get shot," Rita warned.

"Then why don't you lock the door?"

"I don't need to! You need to knock or call to let somebody know you walkin in. And if you can't do that, announce yourself. We got children in here."

"Alright Momma," Keleya said impassively. She placed her purse in a kitchen chair and asked Stacy how she was doing.

"Fine, I'm little tired though," Stacy replied as she placed another hunk of cake in her mouth. She was worn from her monthly, three-hour drive from Nashville.

Keleya locked the wrought iron storm door before grabbing her niece's bracelet and entering the den. The children were making a makeshift fort by draping sheets over the furniture. "Hey Auntie," Janya said excitingly. Jayden and Jayla acknowledged their aunt with a smile, but they were more focused on play.

"Hey Smurf. I remade your bracelet." Keleya sat on the couch and motioned for Janya to come over.

Janya stood in front her aunt, placing one hand on Keleya's knee while the bracelet was placed across her tiny wrist. "Mommy told me you and Kris broke up."

"Is that right?" 'Who the hell tells a five-year-old about their aunt's break up?' Keleya immediately thought. "And what did your mommy say?" Keleya asked sweetly. She didn't want Janya to feel at fault.

"That you don't live together anymore."

"Give me a hug and go play," Keleya directed. She'd heard enough.

As she moved away, Janya announced, "I'm spendin the night. We havin a slumber party in here with Granny."

"That'll be fun…Jayden and Jayla, y'all didn't give me a hug." The six-year-old and three-year-old rushed over, hugged their aunt and continued to drape as if they were never interrupted.

Just as Keleya was about to kick off her shoes and assume a comfortable position, her mother shouted her name. "Leya! Your phone in here ringin!"

Upon walking in the kitchen and hearing the ring, Keleya knew it was JaCola. She picked up the phone and re-entered the den. "What's up girl?"

"Hey, what you doing?" JaCola asked.

"Over Rita house. Where you at?"

"Leavin work. I'm bout to stop and get me somethin to eat. You gone be busy later?"

"No, why?"

"I was gone come over and show you our pictures."

"You got them back already?" Keleya asked.

"Yep, picked them up this mornin."

"Well don't come over til after 6:00. I should be back home by then."

"Yes, can I get a number two with no onions...okay, I'll see you later. I'm tryin to order my food," JaCola said quickly to end the call.

"Alright." Just as Keleya got off the phone, Rita called her name again. Keleya could tell by the tone in her mother's voice that she expected her to come to the kitchen, but Keleya didn't feel like leaving the room. She ignored her mother and continued to watch SpongeBob SquarePants, listening to her nieces and nephew fuss about who owned the fort.

"Keleya!" Rita screamed. Keleya finally got up and walked to the kitchen. "Leya come over here and sit down so we can talk." Keleya didn't want to sit, but she sat across from her mother. And as soon as she sat down, Rita stood to place a plate in the sink. She returned to her seat and folded her arms. "Why you let Kris and that girl tear your apartment up and not do nothin about it?"

Keleya rolled her eyes to the ceiling. Then she glanced at Stacy who was nibbling on cake crumbs as a pretext for listening to forthcoming conversation. "There's nothin to do about it."

"Yes there is. You don't let *nobody* do you like that Leya... have y'all talked about it?"

"No. And ain't no y'all to it."

"Umm," Rita grunted. "Kris ain't came back to the

apartment yet?"

"No, it's done with." Keleya didn't see a need to say anything about their meeting tomorrow.

"See…that's why you can't mess around with females," Stacy commented. "It never ends well."

"Who asked you?" Keleya snapped.

"I'm just sayin," Stacy replied. "Kris obviously thinks she can do certain things and intimidate you just cause ya'll female. If you were a man, she wouldn't have done that."

"What does the fact that Kris and I are women got to do with anything Stacy? And what's this intimidate crap? Shit happens." Keleya looked Stacy dead in her face, but her sister did not respond. Then she thought about the profanity she'd just used in their mother's presence. But because Rita was silent on the matter, Keleya figured she didn't mind in this case.

"I just think that—"

"I don't care what you think Stacy!" Keleya wasn't fond of her sister's heterosexist, high-and-mighty ideals.

"You may not want to hear what—"

"Stacy," Rita interjected. "Let me talk to your sister for a minute." Stacy immediately rose from the table, placed her plate in the sink and walked into the den. Rita kept her eyes on Stacy until she was out of sight. "Now Keleya…you know I ain't never cared about you likin or being with a woman." 'That's a lie,' Keleya thought. "But this done went too far. I never thought that Kris would do somethin like that, but I forgot you can't put nothin past nobody." Keleya recalled those were the same words that Nkosazana used. "Now if you think you gone be safe and Kris and that girl not gone come back round there, then I'll leave it alone." Keleya stared at the table and scratched her arm. "You ain't got nothin to say?"

After a few seconds, Keleya looked at her mother. "If Kris was a man would you feel the same way?" she asked as plainly as possible.

Rita sat back in the chair. She exhaled and said, "Yes."

I was confused. I wasn't sure if Momma said yes to appease me or if she actually meant it. I wanted to trust in her response. But I knew deep down that if Kris were male, Momma would be bothered by what he'd done to me, but she would not view it as a good enough reason to completely cease our four year and one month relationship. She would instead be more concerned about the fact that her daughter had found a good man—an attractive, respectable and educated man—and was letting him go. I knew Momma didn't give a damn about the fact that I'd found a good woman and was letting her go.

• • •

Keleya could hear JaCola's car pulling up outside. She cracked the door and hoped that JaCola would make a quick entrance so the mosquitoes would not enter the apartment too. JaCola has always been very affectionate, so she walked in and gave her best friend a hug. After sitting, she pulled the photographs from her oversized Gucci knock off. The photos were in a suede-like album and featured JaCola and her son at various scenic locations in Memphis. "These are nice Cola," Keleya commented as she turned the page. "She did a real good job...look at Maleek. He's sooo cute...where y'all take this one at?"

"At the park by my house," JaCola answered.

"Really? I don't remember it lookin like that."

"That's cause they cut the grass and planted some trees."

"Umm...it definitely looks better...where's Maleek?"

"He with his daddy...where the scissors at so I can cut you some of these?"

"In the top drawer next to the frigerator."

JaCola got up and walked to the kitchen while Keleya continued to flip through the album. She shut the drawer and turned to walk back to the couch, suddenly noticing the mask on the wall. "Leya, what happened to that?"

"Happened to what?"

"That," JaCola pointed.

Keleya looked at JaCola in order to see what she was referencing. "Oh! Damn, I forgot about that. It fell off the wall the other day."

"And broke on the couch?" JaCola questioned.

"Yeah," Keleya said reassuringly. JaCola knew that Keleya was bullshitting, but she moved on and asked Keleya which pictures she preferred.

For the next two hours, the friends drank Moscato as they talked about JaCola's experience with a freelance photographer...Maleek...his father...various reality television shows...work drama...family drama...and a possible trip to Las Vegas. "You want another glass?" Keleya asked.

"Yeah, but don't give me too much," JaCola stated. As Keleya passed the next round, JaCola asked, "What happened to the mask? And where is Kris? Cause I been here for over two hours and she ain't walked through the door or called you." JaCola was aware of the fact that you could not push Keleya to open up, but her low tolerance for alcohol waned her restraint and understanding for Keleya's personality.

Keleya inhaled and then exhaled. "Kris broke it."

JaCola was taken aback and quiet for a moment. "Where is she?"

"I don't know. I figured she stayin with her momma or sister."

"What the hell happened?" Since the incident was no longer a secret, Keleya explained to JaCola the whole story... the club...the text messages...the argument...the broken mask...She even told JaCola about the next day's meeting with Kris. "I can't believe she did that! When I came in I noticed things looked a lil different, but I didn't think nothin about it til I saw the mask. But you know Kris didn't break it cause that would be low down. I mean all of it was low down, but that's got Dréa written all over it."

"JaCola please! Kris didn't just sit back and let her cousin fuck up our apartment. She did it too." Keleya ran her fingers through her hair and looked at the floor. Then she glanced at the coffee table, now covered with a piece of multi-color fabric. She decided to pull the fabric back to reveal Dréa's calligraphy.

"Uh uhh! That's fucked up! And the mask too! I'd be kickin somebody's ass! Damn girl. See you better than me cause I would've called my cousins up. You should've...." At this point, JaCola entered the bathroom for the third time. Though the bathroom door was closed, Keleya could hear JaCola rambling about what she should have done and what she still could do. Then she came out, strangely calm, and sat beside Keleya. "Seriously Leya, are you okay?"

"I'm fine," Keleya replied.

"So what does that mean?" JaCola asked loudly. "You still wanna be with Kris even after what she did to you?"

"The way that I feel about her hasn't changed Cola...but we don't need to be together right now."

"Daaamn, y'all used to be, like, the happiest couple I knew...hell, at one point I thought she had replaced me," JaCola laughed.

Keleya smiled, but she had long felt that JaCola held a vicarious sentiment for her relationship with Kris. "Well... you know me and Kris always been friends. Even when we initiated the relationship our friendship never went away." Keleya paused to place her legs on the couch. "The problem is that we're not in school anymore...we moved back, got this apartment…I got a job but Kris struggled for months to find a job and that caused a lot of tension…but the main issue is that being in school and livin together while in school drove our relationship. Comin back here took all that away and things changed."

"So…why y'all gettin together tomorrow? And why on Valentine's Day? Don't you think that's a little weird? Who chose the day? Kris?"

"Cola, you just asked me like four or five questions. And no, I chose the day cause I don't give a fuck about it being Valentine's Day. Plus, I was at my momma's house today. And the only reason I'm going is because she asked…and I guess it's a way to show her that I don't have hard feelings."

"I don't know how you couldn't…but you do you," JaCola stated. Keleya looked away and shrugged her shoulders. "What you gone say?"

"I'm gone say somethin about the mask…and she got some stuff over here that she needs to get…and I need the keys she got to my car and this apartment."

"What if she says she wants ya'll to be together?"

"I don't think she will."

"Do you want her to apologize?"

Keleya didn't answer right away. She hadn't really considered it, so she thought about it for several seconds. "I don't like when people apologize for shit they know they shouldn't have done in the first place…I don't want anything from Kris."

"You wanna be friends?"

Keleya shook her head and said, "I don't know."

I wish I had definitive answers for both JaCola and myself. But I really didn't know what I wanted the status of my relationship to be with Kris…so tomorrow should be telling.

February 26th

WITH THE EXCEPTION of text messages, almost two weeks had passed since Keleya and JaCola last talked. So JaCola invited Keleya out for dinner. The pair decided to meet at Carson's.

JaCola brought her older sister Angie along on the outing, but Keleya didn't mind. Keleya and Angie became mutual friends in middle school after Angie squashed a brawl between JaCola and a bully. It was rumored throughout their childhood—mostly by JaCola—that Angie secretly crushed on Keleya, but Angie always denied it. Keleya and JaCola, however, became instant friends the first day of fourth grade. Ever since that day, they grew to learn the many similarities they shared, such as living in a single parent household, having sisters around the same age, related personalities, and similar likings in food, colors and smells. And as they became older, they both grew into young women who fell in love. The only difference was that JaCola got pregnant and Keleya couldn't. "Damn Keleya, I ain't seen you in a minute. What you been up to?" Angie asked with a smile.

"Nothin. How you been?" Keleya asked, thinking about how Angie had gravitated toward a much more masculine demeanor.

"I been a'ight. Tryin to stay out of trouble and stack some paper," Angie said while rubbing her hands together.

"And how is that?" JaCola asked. Before Angie could refute her sister's question, the waiter approached the table again for orders. JaCola ordered first. "I wanna get the The Trio with boneless buffalo wings, mozzarella sticks and potato skins…and ranch."

"Would you like an entrée as well or just the appetizer?" the waiter asked.

"Just the appetizer," she replied.

He acknowledged Angie next. "Can I get The Carson, well done, and no salt on the fries?

"Anything else with the burger?"

"Naw, that's it," Angie replied.

"Can I get an order of classic buffalo wings and an order of boneless buffalo wings both with ranch. And can you bring us a big stack of napkins, please?" Keleya requested.

"No problem. I will have your orders out as soon as they are up."

As soon as the waiter left, JaCola and Angie burst into laughter. "Damn you can eat," JaCola stated.

"And what's up with the napkin request?" Angie asked.

"Leave me alone," Keleya smiled. "Angie where you livin at now?"

"Far. In Olive Branch."

"She livin in Mississippi with some scallywag," JaCola commented.

Angie looked at JaCola and shoved her with her elbow. "She don't live with me." Then she looked at Keleya and said, "I heard you broke up with your girl."

JaCola quickly looked out the window as if she didn't hear her sister's comment. "Yeah…didn't work out," Keleya said before kicking JaCola's foot under the table.

"You lookin for somebody?" Angie asked. "I got a friend you should meet."

"Angie, uh uhh. I just got out of a relationship. Can I be single for a month please?"

The waiter approached the table again with a second glass of Long Island Iced Tea for JaCola. "Your orders should be coming up in a few."

"Thanks," JaCola said. She took a few long sips and turned her attention to Keleya. "So...we ain't had a chance to talk about what happened last Sunday. What ya'll talk about?"

Keleya figured she might as well tell JaCola now because she would only ask again later. "Not much to be honest."

"She try to get back with you?" JaCola asked.

"No...she just went on and on about how sorry she was for what her and Dréa had done, and how she knew that she could never do anything to replace the mask, and that Dréa broke it before she could stop her, and that Dréa wrote that shit in the table when she went into the room to get clothes and that she wanted us to be friends."

"Did she apologize for sleepin with that girl?"

"Nope. And when I said somethin about it she did everything she could to avoid it."

"Umm...did she bring you anything for Valentine's Day?"

Keleya laughed and said, "No she didn't."

"That's the least her ass could have done!" JaCola stated. She waited until after the server placed all the plates before proceeding with her next comment. "Well...y'all can be friends with benefits cause ain't nothin wrong with keepin that good yank around," JaCola said grinning from ear to ear.

"Cola what's up with you tonight? First you tell your sister all my bu'iness and now you..." Keleya couldn't finish her sentence on account of JaCola's sudden laughter.

Angie looked annoyed. "Damn girl, sit back and drink

this." She handed her sister a glass of ice water and grabbed the Long Island Iced Tea to take a quick sip. "This is full of alcohol and you know she can't hold no liquor."

"Who you tellin?" Keleya agreed. "Give that drink to that man when he comes back around here."

"Umm, hold up!" JaCola objected. "I'm payin for this!" She reached over Angie to take the Iced Tea back.

"JaCola chill out," Angie said lowly and slowly.

JaCola placed the tea next to the water, sat upright in her chair, adjusted the black hat on her head and rest her hands on the table. "Are ya'll really through with each other? You don't plan on talking to her again?" she asked, carefully enunciating each word as to not appear tipsy.

At first, Keleya was puzzled. She'd forgotten that JaCola knew nothing of her frequent contact with Kris since Valentine's Day. "No, I didn't say that."

"Sooo…what the hell is that supposed to mean?"

"We're going out on the fourth."

"Hold the fuck up!" JaCola yelled as she slapped her hand on the table. "You gone let her take you out for your birthday?"

"She asked."

JaCola shook her head and rolled her eyes in disapproval. "Leya, I know that's yo girl and you care for Kris and shit, but I ain't never took you for a woman that would let her girlfriend fuck around…you should have said no."

"What's the big deal with Kris takin me out Cola?"

JaCola didn't answer. She turned to Angie and asked, "What you think?"

"I ain't in it. That's a grown ass woman. She can do what she wanna do," Angie replied before biting into her burger.

JaCola rolled her eyes and looked at Keleya. "Mark my words, she gone slowly work her ass back in."

Keleya exhaled and smiled. "JaCola, I love you, but you gettin on my nerves."

Keleya, JaCola and Angie continued to talk while eating, reminiscing and laughing. Before parting ways, JaCola reminded Keleya that her 26th birthday was soon approaching and that they would get together to make more plans.

Plans? I didn't know what JaCola was talking about because this was the first time she'd brought up a party. And what was I supposed to contribute? Even though I knew JaCola wouldn't remember much of this conversation in the morning, I hugged her goodbye and said okay.

March 4th

"HEY, YOU BUSY?" Kris asked.

"No," Keleya replied.

"I was callin to see if we still going out."

"If I didn't wanna go I would have called you Kris."

"What time you leavin work?"

Keleya glanced at the time on the desktop. It was only 1:14. "I get off at 5:00."

"So what time you want me to pick you up?"

"Mmm…it really don't matter. 6:30."

"Alright."

"Okay, bye."

After hanging up the office phone, Keleya sat at her desk and reflected on the short exchange with her ex. It didn't feel or sound any differently than the many times Kris called before. The familiarity was comforting, so comforting that Keleya briefly questioned the termination of their relationship. Then she thought about JaCola's opposition. At 7:00 that morning, JaCola called to wish Keleya a happy birthday. But before ending the conversation, she interjected one last protest to the "birthday date."

Keleya drifted into memories of her last four birthdays, all of which were spent with Kris. When Kris offered to take her out this year, saying yes felt more than natural. So what did JaCola expect her to do? The ring of Keleya's office phone suddenly interrupted her reflection. "C.V.A. this is Keleya," she answered.

"Keleya, there's a delivery for you at the front desk," Jackie, the lobby receptionist said.

"Okay. I'm on my way." Keleya hung up the phone and thought 'delivery?' In the past eleven months, she'd only signed for one package. However, she didn't view this instance as peculiar. Keleya walked out of her shared office and headed to the main hall. As soon as she cut the corner to enter the lobby she saw the deliveryman holding three silver balloons. One read *Happy Birthday*. The others were in the form of the numbers two and six.

"Here comes the birthday girl!" Jackie exclaimed. "Somebody obviously cares about you hun. What are your plans for today?"

"Nothin much. I'm going to dinner with a friend," Keleya replied as she received the balloons and card.

"Well happy birthday and I hope you enjoy the rest of your day," Jackie congratulated.

"Thank you. I'll see you later." Once in the office, Keleya sat the balloons in the corner and opened the card.

Happy 26th Birthday Leya!
We love you!
From Momma, Stacy, Jayden, Jayla, Zana, and Janya

Keleya smiled. Her mother and sisters made a three-way call to tell her happy birthday just after she arrived to work, so the afternoon surprise was highly unanticipated.

After work, Keleya drove directly home. She took a shower and then talked to Janya and her closest cousin, Donyelle, while waiting for Kris. Surprisingly, Kris was on time, so Keleya didn't notice the sound of her car outside. She felt awkward hearing Kris knock on the door. After all, Kris lived there less than a month before. "Hey, you ready?" Kris asked after Keleya opened the door.

"Yeah, let me get my purse." Kris figured that Keleya left the door open as an invitation to step inside. However, she declined and left to wait in the car.

After Keleya got in the Impala, Kris asked, "You decide where you wanna go?"

"Yeah, Olive Garden."

"I offered to take you anywhere and you choose Olive Garden."

"Right. So let's go."

After a short ten-minute drive they arrived at the restaurant. Before proceeding to the entrance, Kris opened the back door to get a package. It was a gift bag for Keleya. "What's in the bag?" Keleya asked.

"You know it's for you so be patient," Kris replied. Keleya and Kris shared a good conversation over dinner. Kris elaborated on her new physical therapy position and her plans to move into a two-bedroom apartment with Dréa over the upcoming weekend. Keleya asked about Kris' family, her niece and nephew in particular. "They a'ight. Bad as hell though."

"No they not," Keleya stated. "Takira and Davian ain't never acted up a day in they life."

"Please. When you around them, they act one way. But when they with me or they momma, it's a whole different story...what about Nya? How she doing?" Kris asked with a smile.

"My baby is good."

"She still got that mouth on her?" Kris asked.

"You know it. She got it honest," Keleya smiled.

"We should get them together and go do somethin.'"

"Yeah we should."

"What about JaCola?"

Keleya smiled. "JaCola is fine."

"What you smilin about?"

"She didn't think it was appropriate for you to ask me out on my birthday," Keleya responded. Kris rolled her eyes and fanned her hand to signify 'whatever'. "Dang, what's all this about?" Keleya asked, replicating Kris' gesture.

"I know that's your bestie, but she too damn overprotective of you," Kris explained. Keleya laughed. "You don't find that shit weird?"

Keleya continued to laugh and said, "No."

"Did your daddy call you today?"

"Who?" Keleya sneered. She corrected Kris by saying, "You mean Momma's sperm donor?"

"Did he?" Kris asked again.

"Has he called in the past?"

"No, but this year could've been different."

"Well it wasn't. Move on," Keleya demanded.

"What about your momma? How she doing?"

"She alright. Same old same."

"Does she know about us?"

"Yes."

"You told her?"

"No."

"Then how did she find out?"

"Think about it Kris."

After she finished chewing and swallowing her chicken alfredo, Kris guessed, "Zana?" Keleya shook her head yes. "What did she say?"

"Let's not get into that right now," Keleya replied.

When they were done with their entrées, Kris handed

Keleya the gift bag. "You can open it now." Keleya looked in the bag and giggled at the sight of her favorite color and candy. Kris bought her two bags of personalized, yellow M&M's. She took the packages out of the gift bag to read the imprinted messages: *Happy Birthday, KRS* and *March 4th.*

"Thanks Kris. You're sweet."

"You like it?"

"Yeah, you knew I would."

"One bag is for you to keep. You can eat the other one." Keleya smiled and thought 'today has been a great day.' So prior to leaving the restaurant, she decided their evening would continue by seeing a movie. They caught a 9:15 flick. "You must not be going to work tomorrow?" Kris asked as they exited the theatre two hours later.

"No, I took off to have an extended weekend. That was my gift to myself. What time you gotta be at work?"

"8:00."

"It's gettin late, you can—"

"No, if there's somethin else you wanna do, let's do it. Don't worry about me. I'm straight."

However, Keleya didn't want anything more so Kris drove her home. Once there, Keleya asked Kris if she wanted to come inside for a minute, but Kris didn't answer. She appeared slightly anxious as she fidgeted with the steering wheel. "What's wrong?" Keleya asked, but Kris was still silent. "Nevermind, I'll talk to you—"

"Leya…I don't understand why you keep avoidin the subject of us."

"There is no us."

"We're not living together, but that doesn't mean my feelings for you have changed. I understand that our relationship has…that it's—"

"Over," Keleya inserted.

"Is that what you really want? You gone sit there and tell me that everything we put into this relationship is over because of one argument?"

"One argument?" Keleya was appalled at the notion. "What we had is over because you lost the trust that I had for you and the respect that I thought you had for me!" After a moment of stillness, Keleya spoke. "Kris, thank you for everything…I'll talk to you later."

Just as Keleya moved to open the car door, Kris placed her hand on Keleya's leg. "Hold on."

"What is it?" Keleya asked with sadness in her voice.

"I'm sorry. I shouldn't have said that…look, at the end of the day, I love you Leya." Kris moved towards Keleya and rubbed her arm, but Keleya didn't respond to her affection. "Can you give me a hug before you leave?" Keleya looked at Kris and leaned across the console to hug her goodbye. Kris placed her arms around Keleya and caressed her back. When Kris released her embrace and stared into Keleya's eyes, she couldn't stop herself from tenderly rubbing the face of the woman she loved. And since Keleya didn't withdraw from her affection, Kris slowly kissed her lips.

When I got in the apartment, I threw my purse and keys on the dining room table and checked the texts that I received in Kris' car. JaCola had sent three texts in the last twenty minutes.

Call me when you get home.
You still out with Kris?
R u home yet!!!

I know I should be careful with the way I feel right now, but I'm not texting her back…JaCola is not about to ruin my high.

March 14th

FOR THE PAST few nights, Keleya laid in her bed unable to fall asleep. At first it didn't bother her, but being in the apartment alone was beginning to feel strange. She cut the TV off and stroked her arm gently and slowly with the tips of her fingers the same way that Kris did.

I haven't talked to Kris since my birthday. I'm a little scared that if she called tomorrow, I'll let her back in my space. I miss companionship... closeness...skin...warmth...touch...I miss her.

April 8th

"COLA, I CAN'T believe you doing all this for your birthday," Keleya stated.

"I know, but I ain't had a party in years," JaCola noted.

"Well...let me know if you need anything cause I'm going to work tomorrow."

"What time you get off?"

"I don't know yet."

"Okay. But I think everything is taken care of. Just show up...and don't sit the whole time. Get up and dance or somethin. Hit that pole up."

"Excuse me? I'll see what I can do," Keleya joked.

"Alright then. Me and my baby bout to go to sleep."

"I'll call you tomorrow."

• • •

Despite Keleya's reluctance to attend her best friend's birthday celebration, she went to the beauty and nail shop the next day after work. Keleya, along with her sister, arrived at *The City* thirty-five minutes after the official start time wearing a chest baring, sleeveless, black, halter dress accompanied with black, five inch peek toe pumps. After passing security, the sisters proceeded upstairs to VIP. Keleya's goal was to speak, hand JaCola her gift and then find a seat, whereas Nkosazana's mission was to scan and locate bachelors.

Once on the second level, Keleya recognized only a few of JaCola's family members. After spotting Angie, they walked in her direction. Keleya tried to get Angie's attention by calling her name, but the music was too loud. So she approached Angie from behind and touched her arm. Angie turned around holding a glass with brown liquor and said, "Hey miss lady. I was wonderin when you was gone get here." She embraced Keleya and held a few seconds too long for comfort. Before releasing the hold on Keleya's lower back, she whispered in her ear, "Damn you smell good. And you look even better."

Keleya took a half step backwards and said thank you in a sort of unpleasant manner. "You remember Zana don't you?"

"Hell yeah," Angie said loudly as she hugged Nkosazana. "How you been?"

"Good," Nkosazana replied. "What you got in that glass?"

"Just a little Coke and Hennessey. I like my shit old school. Go get you a drink, the bar right over there."

"We don't want no bar. Where's your sister?" Keleya demanded.

"Damn, why yo sister so mean?" Angie asked. Nkosazana smiled and shrugged her shoulders. "Hell, she over there somewhere," Angie said, motioning with the glass. As Keleya turned to walk away, Angie stepped in her path. "You gone dance with me later?"

"No," Keleya said with a no nonsense expression.

"Just one dance baby."

Keleya knew that acceding to the request would be enough to get Angie out of her face, so she said yes and walked away. Keleya and Nkosazana found JaCola near the balcony railing, sitting at a large booth with a tabletop full of shot glasses and several bottles of Grey Goose. As soon as she saw Keleya, JaCola rushed to her friend with a big hug. Nkosazana said happy birthday and JaCola hugged her too. "Why ya'll so late?" JaCola asked.

"We ain't late," Keleya said to avoid hurting JaCola's feelings. "We just got through talkin to Angie."

"She drunk yet?"

"Oh yeah."

"You look good," JaCola commented.

Keleya studied JaCola for a second. She'd forgotten how revealing JaCola's birthday outfit would be. "Thanks Cola."

"Did you see my momma?"

"No. She actually came?"

"Yeah, she was up here a minute ago."

"Let me know when she comes back cause I ain't seen her in a minute," Keleya requested. But her request seemed to fall on deaf ears when JaCola started to dance. "Girl, you listenin to me?"

"Yeah baby," JaCola replied. Like Angie, she called everyone baby. JaCola turned around to grab two shots from the booth—one for Keleya and one for Nkosazana. "Here y'all go."

"I don't want that," Keleya said. Nkosazana, however, accepted the shot of vodka.

"Well then me and Zana will drink these," JaCola stated. And they did. Afterwards, Keleya sat at a nearby table and Nkosazana and JaCola followed. "Leya I told you I didn't want you sittin down all night."

'You should be glad I'm here,' Keleya thought. 'And I came lookin good.' "Cola, you know I comes to chill."

"And what did you come to do?" JaCola asked Nkosazana.

"I came to have a good time girl." Nkosazana stood from the table and said, "I'll be back."

"Cola as long as you're enjoyin this, that's all that matters," Keleya commented.

"Thank you and I am. But dance before it's over, okay?"

"I might."

Nkosazana returned with a lime-garnished mojito. Before sitting, she grabbed a shot from the booth. "Here, loosen up," she said as she placed the glass in front of her sister.

"No. I'm good."

"Leya," Nkosazana said frustratingly.

"What's up with ya'll tryin to force alcohol on me tonight?" Keleya picked up the glass and poured the majority of the vodka into Nkosazana's beverage. She then drank the remainder. "Happy now?" Nkosazana looked at her sister with a hell-no look on her face. "You should be cause I'm yo driver."

Nkosazana ignored her sister and asked JaCola, "You know any single men over twenty-five, preferably thirty in here?"

JaCola was too tipsy to say much, so she only replied, "Yeah."

"From what I seen, the only thing you gone potentially get out of here is a fuck or a STD," Keleya commented.

"Well, I'll take a good fuck," Nkosazana said while checking her phone for texts.

"I didn't say good," Keleya responded.

"Look, I'll be back." Nkosazana stood again, this time placing her purse directly in front of Keleya. "Watch this for me." She left with cell phone in hand.

Keleya placed her sister's bag in the adjacent chair and then looked at JaCola who was obviously reaching her limit. But before Keleya could ask if she was okay, JaCola's mother Desirée—better known as Buggy—came to the table. Keleya had always liked JaCola's mother. She was touchy–feely, but nice. Buggy hugged Keleya before sitting down and introducing a few family members—many whom she'd actually met years before. JaCola didn't stay around for most of the conversation. Keleya figured she was too embarrassed to be intoxicated in front of her mother, but it wasn't like the woman didn't know or couldn't tell. Angie eventually approached the table and sat next to Keleya. "Y'all need to slow down with the drinkin," Buggy admonished Angie.

"Momma we a'ight. We just havin a little fun…and we payin for it."

"Ain't no we," Buggy retorted.

Angie just smiled and sipped. "Can I have my dance now?"

"Dance?" Keleya asked as if she had no clue what Angie meant.

"So it's like that?"

"Go on Keleya," Buggy encouraged. "This the kind of music y'all young folks like. Get on out there. As much as you and Cola used to be in my backyard shakin around. I *know* you can dance."

"No ma'am. I'm stayin right here."

"Why not?" Buggy asked.

"My shoes," Keleya said, poking her right foot from under the table so that Buggy could view the high-heeled shoe.

"If you wore em, you can work with em. Go on…I'll watch your stuff," Buggy smiled. However, Keleya wasn't fooled by her blithe presence. This wasn't the first time that Buggy had attempted to initiate a love connection between her daughter and Keleya.

Keleya hesitated but eventually stood, placing her phone, keys and sister's purse in the seat. "I'm leavin it right here," she pointed. Buggy continued to beam as Keleya and Angie walked away.

Angie took Keleya's hand and led the way to the club's dance floor. *The City* catered to a mixed crowd, primarily because of the same–sex orientation of one of the three club owners. This indeed contributed to the club's popularity and revenue. JaCola befriended Cardell, one of the co-owners, nearly a year ago—hence her party location. Before heading downstairs, they passed JaCola. She was elated to see her friend and sister hand–in–hand so she waved. Keleya gave her a smile and the finger in return. Once on the main level and at the dance floor, Angie pulled Keleya close and asked how she was feeling. "I'm good Angie."

"Then why you so uptight?" Angie asked. She glanced at Keleya's full cleavage and stated, "If you come in here lookin ripe, you will be devoured."

"Angie, please. And I'm not uptight. I'm being myself and you know it." Angie smiled because she knew Keleya was right. She then moved in closer, so close that Keleya noticed the *A & T* tattooed on her lower neck. Keleya consumed herself so much in reflecting on the when and why of the acronym that she didn't notice how tightly Angie began to hold her. She remembered that Angie got the tattoo nearly five years ago and that *A & T* stood for *Ass and Tits*, two things Angie always claimed she loved most in life. After a moment, Keleya noticed Angie was all over her ass. She pushed her body away and said "Angela" with a firm voice.

"My fault," Angie said as she came to her senses.

They talked and danced to only a few more songs because Keleya grew tired of trying to maintain boundaries between them. As the last song ended, Keleya said, "Angie, I enjoyed this. Deuces."

"Damn baby don't leave yet."

"You can stay here or come with me," Keleya directed.

"I need to talk to you."

"About what?" Keleya asked as she turned to go back upstairs. But she didn't stop to acknowledge Angie until back at the table. "What is it?" Keleya asked after sitting.

Angie waited a moment for her mother to leave before proceeding. "I know it ain't been that long since you ended things with Kris, but I got somebody I want you to meet."

"No!"

"Daaamn…come on now. Y'all should meet."

Keleya didn't want Angie to get the wrong impression from her reaction, but the matchmaking offer was so amusing all she could do was laugh. "Angie thank you, but no," Keleya smiled. "I'm not ready to be involved with nobody in any kind of way right now."

"How long has it been since ya'll broke up?" Angie asked.

'Two months,' Keleya thought. "It don't matter."

"Do you think I'd introduce you to some fucked up woman?"

"Yes." They both laughed. "Angie, no! Plus I'm shy."

"Shy people don't dress like that."

Keleya rolled her eyes. "Ten minutes ago you were all over me and now you tryin to push me onto somebody else."

Angie laughed, pointed to her neck and said, "A and T baby. A and T."

Keleya smiled. "Whatever."

"Seriously though. I got a friend. She in here somewhere. Y'all should talk."

"Oh my god. Please don't tell me you been tellin some chick in here that—"

"Naw, it ain't like that. I knew both of ya'll would be here tonight, so I told her I might introduce the two of you." Keleya rubbed her forehead and then her hair. She wasn't feeling the proposition. "You wanna meet her?" Angie smiled. "You gone be nice?" she asked more seriously.

"I'm only not nice to you."

"Yes or no?"

Keleya tapped her fingernails on the tabletop. "Okay," she reluctantly agreed.

"Hold on a second." Angie stepped to the booth for three shots. She swallowed one and left the others on the table. "Look don't leave, I'll be back."

After Angie left, Keleya started to feel a little nervous tension. She quickly and semi–secretly downed one of the shots while waiting. In the meantime, JaCola made her rounds again, this time more sober. Twelve minutes into their chat, Keleya saw Angie re-enter VIP accompanied with a stranger. She considered taking the other shot of vodka, but as they drew closer she reconsidered. "Do you know this person your sister is introducin me to?"

"Who you talkin about?" JaCola asked. Keleya motioned for her to look back. JaCola turned around and said, "Yeah."

"What's her name?"

"You'll find out when she gets over here."

"Cola don't play."

"I don't remember. I just met her tonight Leya. Angie invited her."

"And?"

"And nothin."

"Why you and Angie schemin?"

"Leya," JaCola laughed, "I don't know no more than you. And that's the truth." Keleya didn't believe her, but it was too late to pry more information from her because Angie and the friend were now approaching the table. "Hey, have a seat," JaCola said.

Angie took a seat in front of her sister and this *very* attractive sister sat in front of Keleya. So instead of waiting for Angie to start introductions, Keleya took the initiative. She extended her right hand and said, "Hey, I'm Keleya."

"What's up? I'm J."

Just as Keleya was about to begin her next statement, Angie cut her off by standing and saying, "Umm…mission accomplished. So we gone leave y'all here to get to know one another." JaCola smiled, winked and left with her sister.

Keleya looked at J. "This is a little awkward."

"True…but it doesn't have to be," J said with a smile. And when she smiled, Keleya *really* paid attention. She thought about how cute Angie's friend turned out to be. Actually, cute didn't seem befitting. J was handsome, but in a charmingly feminine way.

Keleya looked at her smooth lips and into her bright brown eyes again and asked, "Is your name actually J or does it stand for somethin embarrassing like Joanne?"

J laughed. "No, it's Jordan."

"Well, I'll refer to you the way that you introduced yourself."

"Whichever you prefer, I don't mind."

'I guess Cola and Angie know me better than I thought,' Keleya said to herself while thinking about J's sharp, northern accent and melodic voice. "I have a question that I hope you don't mind answering, Jordan."

"No, go ahead," Jordan said, placing her hands palms up to welcome the question.

"What did Angie say about me? I'm curious."

"Nothin. She just invited me and said there would be someone she may introduce me to. She didn't tell me your name or anything," Jordan said before taking a sip of Budweiser.

"Okay…so how do you know each other? Because it doesn't sound like you're from around here."

"Naw, I'm from Philly. And me and Angie work together."

Keleya immediately recalled that Angie worked at The Urvine House. "Okay."

"From time to time when I see Angie at work we talk

about women and relationships. I told her that I wasn't into blind dating and shit, but she insisted that we meet." Jordan reached across the table, rubbed across the top of Keleya's hand and said, "I'm glad we did."

Keleya felt silly for glancing at her hand and smiling, so she asked another question to conceal that she was enjoying the flirtation. "How long you been in Memphis?"

"Almost a year."

"What brought you—?"

"Why don't you let me ask some of the questions now," Jordan interrupted.

Keleya laughed. "Okay."

"How long have you known Angie?"

"About…fifteen, sixteen years."

"So you and JaCola are friends?"

Keleya shook her head yes. "That's my girl. She's like a sister."

"So that makes you what? Twenty-five, twenty-six?"

"Twenty-six." Keleya was on the verge of asking Jordan her age, but Nkosazana returned.

"Hey, I forgot you were here," Keleya commented.

Nkosazana ignored the comment and took a seat. "And who is this?" she smiled.

"Jordan, this is my sister Zana. Zana this is Jordan. We just met, courtesy of Angie."

"Really?" Nkosazana grinned. "Nice to meet you Jordan."

"You too," Jordan replied.

"I don't mean to be rude, but I need to talk to my sister for a second." Nkosazana stood and pointed to the back corner of the room, a place where they could talk in private.

"No problem," Jordan said.

Keleya stood and followed Nkosazana. "What's wrong?" she asked, but Nkosazana didn't speak until they were alone.

Nkosazana turned around and looked past her sister's shoulder. "Girl she is starin you down. What's up with ya'll?"

"I know you didn't bring me over here to ask me that."

"No I didn't. But you can answer me first."

"You let me know what's going on and I may."

Nkosazana considered it for a second. "I need you to do me a favor."

"What?"

"I need you to pick Nya up in the morning from Momma's if I can't make it." She believed her sister would never say no to anything concerning Janya.

"What do you mean if you can't make it? You need…" It suddenly occurred to Keleya what her sister had requested. "Who is it?"

"Don't worry bout all that."

"Don't you think it's a little irresponsible to leave with somebody you don't know?"

Nkosazana adjusted her left bra strap. "Who said I don't know him? And don't worry about me boo. I'm grown." Keleya turned around and headed for the table. "You didn't give me an answer!"

Keleya gave a half turn and shouted, "No!" When she got to the table, she looked back to see if her sister was still there, but Nkosazana had left. She was a little upset and wanted a change of space. So she grabbed her keys from the tabletop and looked at Jordan. "You wanna go to the bar?"

"Sure." Jordan stood and followed her to the bar. Keleya wasn't sure if it was the shot of vodka, the bottle of Smirnoff she was drinking or Jordan's down to earth aura that allowed her to let her guard down a bit. Whatever the case, they talked for over an hour. And they had a good conversation going before JaCola's disruption. But instead of picking up were they left off, Keleya decided that she was ready to leave. She asked

JaCola if there was anything she needed before departing and JaCola said no. Jordan decided to make her exit as well and said goodbye to JaCola. Then she offered to walk Keleya outside.

As they walked to the exit and into more light, Keleya began to fully notice Jordan. She was about five foot, seven inches, lean, smoothly browned skinned, and she walked with a stride of confidence. Once outside, Jordan gave Keleya a short hug as she commented about enjoying the night's meeting and talk.

"I did too," Keleya smiled. "I've never thought that Angie had good taste in women, but she apparently chooses well for others." Jordan laughed. "So…"

"You wanna get together sometime?" Jordan asked spontaneously.

"Mmm," Keleya said slowly. "Maybe."

"Maybe? Is that because you're spendin your time with someone else?"

Keleya smiled. "No."

"Well?" Jordan asked as she took a step toward Keleya.

"Yeah. That'll be cool." Jordan handed Keleya her iPhone and she added her contact information with ease. Keleya handed the phone back and said, "Later."

After I got home and in the bed, I felt kind of bad and immature for what I had done. I'm sure Jordan would trip when she looked under my name to find that I gave her my email address, not my number…but then again, I don't feel that bad. If she's serious about wanting to see me again—or talk to me for that matter—she'll email.

April 14th

SLOW DOWN," JACOLA said panting. "You know I can't go as fast as you."

"I'll slow down, but we're not stoppin…keep going til we get to that bench up there," Keleya stated. As they completed the three-mile power walk and approached the bench, JaCola begged to sit down. Keleya advised her to stay on her feet and to keep moving, but JaCola bent over to rest her hands on her knees. "Get up. You need to stretch."

"Damn girl I'm tired!" JaCola said irritated.

"I know, but you gotta push through it." Keleya was helping JaCola get in better shape. Since Maleek's birth, she'd slowly packed on extra pounds and was no longer content with her figure.

After stretching JaCola asked, "Can we sit down now?"

"Go ahead."

"Bout time," JaCola said as she flopped on the bench. After her heart rate and breathing settled, she looked at Keleya. "I been meanin to ask you if you talked to Kris."

Keleya looked off into the distance. "Yeah." Although it took Kris nearly two weeks to contact Keleya after her birthday, the two had been in frequent contact since.

"So she finally called you?"

"Mmm hmm. Talked to her on Monday," Keleya replied, neglecting to inform her friend of the prior conversations. "And her sister called me when I left work on Tuesday cause she needed somebody to help her take her micros down."

"Did you go?"

"No…I lied and told her I had a work event to go to. I felt bad for doing it, but I'm not with her sister anymore. I know that don't mean that I gotta cut her off completely, but…I would've been uncomfortable over there."

JaCola shook her head in understanding. "So what's the business with you and Kris?"

"We're gettin together Saturday."

"Are you serious?"

"What? Am I not supposed to talk to her or be around her just because we're not together?"

JaCola didn't respond to the question. Instead she asked, "What ya'll plan on doing?"

"We're takin Janya, Takira and Davian to the movies and Cici's…you want me to take Maleek?"

"Naw, he'll be with his daddy folks this weekend. Thanks for askin though."

"What's done happened that all of the sudden Mike done had a change of heart and is spendin time with the child he claimed wasn't his?"

"Girl, I don't know. But if he gone try to do what's right I'm gone let him…I forgot how crazy Janya is about Kris."

"Yeah. When she came over last Saturday she asked me if Kris was comin over too."

"What you tell her?"

"I told her I'd see if she would come next time. But I don't have to worry about that now cause she'll see her Saturday."

"So…Kris ain't said nothin about gettin back together?"

"No. I think she's past that."

"Are you?"

"I'm tryin to be."

"Why? Cause you met Jordan?"

"Cola, I ain't talked to that girl."

"Ya'll ain't talked? Shit, I can't believe that."

It had been four days since JaCola's party, but Keleya hadn't told her about the email address thing yet. "If she do, she do. If she don't, she don't."

"Keleya please! You need to lay off that I don't give a damn shit. You know you want that girl to call you. I could tell you liked her. And stop bullshittin like you don't be thinkin bout Kris. You know you love that girl."

Keleya laughed a little and said, "I never said I didn't… and don't be tryin to get on my case! Do I talk about how you and Cardell keep tip toeing around a nonexistent relationship?"

JaCola laughed and tried to scratch through her quick weave. "Girl, he ain't ready. So he can just keep doing what he do best."

"Umm…well at least you ain't settling. Wish I could say the same for Zana."

"Yo sister is off the chain!"

"Who you tellin? She'll sleep with anybody. And I don't like that shit cause she brings the men around Smurf…that girl gone hoe til she die."

"Leya, that's mean. That's your sister."

"I know, but it's the truth."

"You think she's a nymph?"

"Probably…I just tell her to be careful and to keep Nya away from it…really, I don't know what's wrong with her."

"We all have sex…she just needs to slow down," JaCola noted.

"Right, but it's different when you do it because of a sustained attraction or relationship with the person. Her shit is just random." Keleya looked over at JaCola. "You tired? You ready to go?"

"Yeah, it's time for me to go get my baby."

On my way home, I thought about JaCola and our friendship. She's always been a good listener. And even though she ain't never had a problem opening her big mouth to tell me when she doesn't agree with me or my choices, she's always been equally supportive. Now that I think about it, this thing with Kris is really the only time that she's put her foot down and aggressively disagreed. But regardless of that, I cannot deny that JaCola has always been a better friend to me than I've ever been to her.

April 15th

STRANGELY ENOUGH, JORDAN emailed Keleya the next day.

10:17 am

Most people would've deleted your name, but I guess I'm different. How are you?

Jordan Alexander, MSW, LCSW
The Urvine House
1705 West Lancaster Court
Memphis, TN 38121
(901) 845-CARE
(901) 845-8665 fax
jalexander@urvine.org

"We're In This Together."

11:19

I'm good Jordan. Sorry about that. Anyway, how are you?
KRS

12:05

*I'm good. I've been thinking about you. You made a
lasting impression.*

Jordan Alexander, MSW, LCSW
The Urvine House
1705 West Lancaster Court
Memphis, TN 38121
(901) 845-CARE
(901) 845-8665 fax
jalexander@urvine.org

"We're In This Together."

1:12

You've been thinking about me for 5 whole days! How is work?
KRS

1:17

*Funny. Work is busy. That's why I didn't get with you sooner. I
wouldn't let a woman as beautiful as you slip out of my life so easily!*

Jordan Alexander, MSW, LCSW
The Urvine House
1705 West Lancaster Court
Memphis, TN 38121
(901) 845-CARE
(901) 845-8665 fax
jalexander@urvine.org

"We're In This Together."

1:31

*Flirting via email. LOL. If you see my girl Angie tell her
I said "Sup!"*
KRS

• • •

10:02 am

*Sorry I didn't get back with you yesterday. Didn't see Angie,
but I may today. I'm a fighter. When I find someone I like,
I go after her. Email is impersonal. I want to hear your voice.
What's your number?*

Jordan Alexander, MSW, LCSW
The Urvine House
1705 West Lancaster Court
Memphis, TN 38121
(901) 845-CARE
(901) 845-8665 fax
jalexander@urvine.org

"We're In This Together."

10:12

No problem. 288–5061. I get off at 5:30.
KRS

That evening, Keleya went home to relax and make earrings. Around 7:15, her phone rang. She answered the call and said hello. "What's up? You at home?" Kris asked.

"Yeah."

"You and Nya still going with us tomorrow."

"Yes. And I hate when you ask me that."

"Ask you what?"

"Am I still this? Or am I still that?" Kris didn't respond to Keleya's pet peeve. "You find out what time the movie starts?"

"2:00. I'll pick y'all up around 1:40 since it's just down the street."

"Okay, we'll be here. I'll see you tomorrow."

"Hold up," Kris said immediately. "Why you rushin me off the phone? What you doing?"

"I thought the conversation was over."

"Why is it that sometimes you talk to me like nothin went down and other times you short as hell?"

'I talk to you when I'm lonely, and when I'm not I ain't got shit to say,' Keleya thought. "Kris, we'll see you tomorrow," she responded and ended the call. Less than a minute later, her phone rang again. Keleya knew it was Kris so she didn't ID the caller. "Hello," Keleya answered, awaiting Kris' reaction.

"Hey, how you doing?"

Keleya didn't recognize the voice. She quickly looked at the touch screen to see the name or number. And after thinking about it for a second, she realized it was Jordan. "I'm good. You threw me off for a second because I wasn't expectin your call. How are you?"

"Good," Jordan replied. "If you're busy I can call you back later."

"No, I'm not busy. I'm glad you called. There are some things I *have* to ask you."

Jordan laughed. "Like what?" Over the next hour and a half and through a series of questions and explanations, Keleya turned her mutual friend status with Jordan into an acquaintanceship. She learned that Jordan was twenty-nine and that she'd moved to Memphis with her mother to care for her grandmother who was sick. Jordan's mother lived with her mother, but Jordan lived in a Midtown apartment. Jordan also shared that her older brother and father still reside in Philadelphia. Then Jordan asked about Keleya's family. Keleya told her about her mother, sisters, nieces and nephew—in addition to her maternal grandmother, who lived outside of Atlanta, and her closest cousin, who lived in Little Rock.

Keleya also asked about Jordan's educational background. Jordan graduated from Penn with degrees in psychology and social work and now worked with girls age nine to twelve as a clinical counselor at The Urvine House, a residential treatment facility for youth in state custody. Keleya explained that she attended The University of Tennessee Knoxville, majoring in journalism and electronic media during undergrad and marketing in grad school. She elaborated on her position as a marketing specialist for The Center for Vocational Activities, a local nonprofit that offered vocational training and job placement assistance to persons with physical and emotional disabilities.

Next, they talked generally about past relationships. Jordan told Keleya about Courtney, whom she'd been with on and off for about three years prior to moving to Memphis. And Keleya told her that she'd recently got out of a relationship. "Do you still see each other?" Jordan asked.

"We talk occasionally."

"Are you friendly?"

"No, we don't have that kind of relationship anymore?"

"So no smashing?"

Keleya laughed. "No."

"If you're unattached can we get together this weekend?"

"We can go out, but this weekend won't work for me."

"You're gonna make me wait til next weekend?"

"You're a fighter, right?"

Jordan laughed. "You're funny...well, if you get the opportunity call me this weekend. If not, call me during the week and let me know what you wanna do." Then she paused and said, "I'll be waiting to hear from you" in the sweetest voice.

Before ending the call, I reassured Jordan that I would get back with her. And because of tonight's conversation, I will.

April 17th

"DAMN DD. YOU can't call me no more?" Keleya asked her cousin.

"Cuzzo, you know more than anybody about being busy," Donyelle responded in her raspy voice. "But I'm good now cause the semester is almost over."

"When you comin to Memphis?"

"I...I don't...I gotta see...I gotta see if my work schedule changes next week."

"What's up with all the pauses? What you doin?"

"I'm tryin to make me somethin eat. You know I can't multi-task."

"I see...let me know when so I can take off."

"I will."

"Hold on DD...Smurf please don't do that. I don't want you to hurt yourself."

"Janya's over there?"

"Yeah. We bout to go to the movies with Kris."

"Kris?"

"Yeah."

"Ya'll together now?"

"No boo, it's strictly platonic."

"Mmm...tell her I said hey."

"Where is Meka?" Keleya asked.

"She at work."

"How things going between ya'll?"

"Good…as far as I know."

"Why you say that?"

"Cause after what happened to you, I say as far as I know."

"DD that's different though."

"Well," Donyelle said while smacking in Keleya's ear, "I like Meka, but she do shit that gets to me."

"Like what?"

"Like…I can't do this, I can't do that. I can't touch her here, I can't touch her there. I ain't gone lie, sometimes I feel like I'm in a relationship with a man."

"You mean cause of her gender?" Keleya asked.

"Yeah…but it's more than that. I don't mind the masculine part. I just can't stand when females start to let that shit determine how they act in *my* relationship."

"I know what you mean. It's one thing to look a certain way because that's what you like. It's another thing to be adoptin shit from straight folks and puttin it in the relationship with your woman. That shit don't fly," Keleya explained.

"Uh huh. Maybe I need to find me somebody like me."

"DD if that's what you like, that's what you like. You just need to find a woman who ain't hell bent on roles."

"Yeah…Kris was never like that was she?" Donyelle asked.

"No, we didn't have that issue. But I did with Toeraysha."

"Toeraysha? Why? She was femme like you."

"That don't mean shit!" Keleya was about to explain the issue to her cousin, but she heard Kris' car outside. "DD, I'll call you back later cause Kris just pulled up."

"Alright then. Love you."

Kris knocked on the door before Keleya could open it. When she opened the door and saw Kris, she almost reconsidered the non-desire she claimed she had for her. Maybe it was the way the golden sun illuminated the warm atmosphere around Kris. Or maybe it was just the fact that she was hell of attractive with killer swag. Whichever, Kris looked damn good and Keleya was pleased to see her. "Ya'll ready?" Kris asked.

"Yeah, we're comin." When Janya realized that Kris was at the door, she ran out of the bedroom and onto the porch.

"What's up Smurf?" Kris asked excitedly. She kneeled down to give her a big hug. "How you been?"

"Good," Janya replied.

Keleya opened the back door of Kris' car for Janya and spoke to Takira and Davian who waited patiently in the back seat. Once in the car, Kris asked the children if they were ready to go. Janya and Takira said yes. Davian said he was hungry. "We'll eat after the movie lil man, okay?" Kris said.

"Okay," Davian complied.

Kris then turned her attention to Keleya and asked, "What's up Leya?"

Keleya looked at Kris and smirked. "I just got off the phone with DD. She said hey."

"What she been up to?"

"Nothin. School and work."

"Why you hang up on me yesterday?"

Keleya crossed her arms. "I was tired."

"Leya, I know you bullshittin."

"Right, I am. So don't ask me again," Keleya said. Kris smiled.

Keleya had a really good time with Kris and especially the children. Although Keleya did not want children of her own while in her twenties, she enjoyed the way they kept her on her toes by questioning everything incorrectly or inaccurately stated. After leaving the pizzeria, Kris took her niece and nephew home. She walked them into her sister's house while Keleya and Janya stayed in the car. "Smurf you look tired. You sleepy now?"

"No," Janya responded. "I think I ate too much."

Keleya laughed. "I think you did too. I told you not to eat all that pizza…you'll be alright though." Kris came back to the car a few minutes later. "Why your sister didn't come out?" Keleya asked.

"She's on the phone. You want me to wait?"

"No, we can leave."

"You want me to drop Nya off?"

"Yeah, let me see if her momma is at home." Keleya pulled the phone out of her purse and noticed a text message, but she decided to read it after calling Nkosazana. "Are you at home?" she asked her sister.

"No."

"Well then how far are you from your house so we can drop Janya off?"

"Can you keep her tonight?"

"No ma'am I cannot. Can you meet us somewhere?"

"Take her over Momma house," Nkosazana said with a blatant attitude.

"Does Momma know she comin over there?"

"I'll call her right quick. Just go ahead and take her over there," Nkosazana demanded. Before Keleya could say anything else, Nkosazana ended the call. Keleya was pissed because she had a strong feeling her sister was indeed at home. She thought about asking Kris to drive there anyway just to confirm her suspicion, but she didn't want to put Janya in a position where she may feel unwanted.

"Am I going to your sister's house?" Kris asked.

"No, go to my momma house…Nya we gone take you to Granny house, okay?"

"Okay," Janya said sleepily. "Is Mommy at home?"

"No."

"Is she at work?" Janya asked.

"I think so."

"You upset?" Kris asked.

"No," Keleya answered quickly.

"Then why you shakin your foot?" At that moment, Keleya stopped. She didn't say anything in response, so Kris reached over to hold her hand for a moment. She knew better than anyone how much love and disgust Keleya held for her sister. When they pulled in Rita's driveway, she was already standing at the carport door waiting. Janya was sleep, so Keleya got out the car to carry her inside. Rita came out the house, of course, to speak and be nosey at the same time. Kris stepped outside the car to say hello. "Hey Ms. Rita."

"Hey Kris. How you been?"

"I been alright."

Rita walked around to the other side of the car. "Wake her up Leya. That girl is too old to be carried," Rita said as she began to shake Janya's arm.

"Momma stop. She alright...Kris I'll be back." Rita said goodbye to Kris and followed Keleya inside.

After Keleya returned to the car, Kris laughed. "Yo momma ain't changed a bit."

"Damn Kris it's only been two months," Keleya laughed. "Maybe I should have made her wake up so she could tell you bye."

"Naw, that's okay. You ready to go home?"

"Yeah, where else am I supposed to be going?" Keleya asked. Kris smiled and shook her head.

While riding to the apartment, Keleya remembered the text she received. She pulled the phone out again to read the message. *Just wanted to say hello n let u know I'm thinkin about u.*

No need to text bk. Keleya couldn't lie to herself. She'd only talked to Jordan twice, but she was feeling her. She thought about calling Jordan later that evening. But in the meantime, she decided to text back. *Ur sweet. Tty soon.*

"Who is that? Your new chick?" Kris asked.

Keleya laughed. "I don't have a new chick."

"Then what you smilin about?"

"The text is from DD and in case you forgot, I'm single." 'You should be the last person questionin me about who I'm seein or doing,' she thought.

"You think I believe that?" Kris stated. "I know you got somebody knockin on your door other than me."

Keleya looked out the window. She didn't feel comfortable sharing with Kris her desire for or attraction to another woman. "No…I don't."

"If you don't wanna tell me that's cool…I wouldn't tell me either if I was you," Kris said sincerely.

The tone of her voice was so familiar. It took Keleya back to a place they'd been many times before. It was the sound of Kris lying in her lap as Kris talked about the strained relationship with her mother because of her same-sex orientation, the hardships of school, childhood molestation and other frustrations as Keleya ran fingers through her locs. At that moment, Keleya longed for a piece of what they used to share. She felt fragile so she changed the subject. "How's your job going?"

"It's okay," Kris answered. "I haven't been there long, but you know that ain't where I really wanna be."

Just as she was about to ask Kris of possible alternatives, they arrived at the apartment. "You wanna come in today?" Keleya asked. After a moment of consideration, Kris accepted the offer.

Keleya sat her purse on the dining room table and walked into the bedroom while Kris stayed in the great room. Kris stood there reflecting on the last time she'd been in the cinnamon scented space. She looked around, noticing the repositioned and redecorated furniture and the new vase on the dining room table. "It looks good in here," Kris stated when Keleya returned.

"Don't even go there," Keleya quickly responded.

"I'm just sayin, you've—"

"Look at that shit," Keleya said pointing to the mask on the wall. Kris didn't look at the mask. Instead, she looked at Keleya, smiled and cast her eyes to the floor. "You think it's funny?"

"No!" Kris said adamantly as she looked at Keleya again. "But I can't lie, your reaction was funny as hell." Keleya responded by looking at Kris with an expression she definitely understood. "Look, on a serious tip," Kris continued, "I smiled because I'm ashamed."

"Let's just leave it alone," Keleya said. She refused to entertain any more feelings or comments about the subject from Kris. "Why you standin up? Sit down."

"I will...it's...weird being in here," Kris replied while taking her hands out of her pockets to rest them on the top of the sectional.

"Why? Because you used to live here or because of the way you left it?"

"Damn Leya. You just said to leave it alone."

"Sit down Kris." After she sat down, Keleya moved to sit adjacent to her. "You know you still got stuff over here."

"You still got it?"

"I just said you got stuff over here. What, you think I was gone channel Angela Bassett on yo ass or somethin?"

Kris laughed. "Maybe...why you keepin it?"

"Because you would eventually get it and it's not in the way...but maybe I should've given you a taste of your own medicine," Keleya said and grinned. "You want somethin to drink?"

"Yeah, what you got?"

"Go see."

"What? You just asked me. You not gone get it for me?"

"No I'm not! I asked to be nice."

Kris laughed and stood while pulling up her pants. "You cold girl."

Keleya and Kris talked and watched TV. Keleya noticed that after a while, Kris relaxed and started to act like her old self again. She got a lot of comfort from Kris being in her space...their old space. She felt like there was never a break in their relationship, and she could tell that Kris felt the same way. But how could they not feel this way? They knew each other better than anyone else. They'd told each other things that no one else knew. They shared a special connection and always would. "Tell me the truth. Who you talkin to right now?" Kris asked.

"Why you keep askin me that Kris? And why do you wanna know?"

"I'm curious...but you ain't gotta tell me. I can call Zana. I still got her number."

While Keleya laughed, Kris leaned over onto her side. She looked at Keleya and licked her lips. "Kris...don't look at me like that."

"Like what?" Kris asked softly.

"You know what I'm talkin about," Keleya responded. She could see the yearning in Kris' eyes.

"I can't reciprocate your feelings?"

"My feelings?"

"Look at me," Kris boasted. "You know you want this."

Keleya laughed. "Kris stop."

"I can't help it. I miss you...come here," Kris whispered, but Keleya ignored her request. "Come here Le Le."

"Oh my god, stop it! And don't call me that," Keleya smiled.

"I wanna be near you. And vice versa, right?" Kris got up and sat next to Keleya. "I don't wanna make you uncomfortable though."

Keleya moved towards Kris and placed her hand on Kris' leg. "You're not."

Before I retracted my hand, Kris rubbed my face and kissed me. She took hold of my hips and pulled me close. Being next to her felt amazing...amazing not because of the physicality, but because of the emotion that swelled inside of me. It was stimulating and satisfying at the same time. I completely let my guard down so that my desires could control me, and they led me to pull her shirt up so that I could place my hands on her lower back. But I wanted to feel more of her silky, caramel skin so I took it off. And she did the same to me. I laid back and Kris gently rubbed my stomach. She kissed the tattoo of our names on my waist and worked her way to my neck. The cooling sensation of her breathe on the slight wetness of my neck was so hypnotizing that I couldn't open my eyes. And when I did, my pants were off and Kris was removing my panties... guess there's no need to call Jordan tomorrow.

April 18th

AFTER EATING BREAKFAST and watching a little TV, Keleya had an urge to write. She felt that writing would be a way to release the feelings that she could not put into clear words or thoughts. She didn't feel bad, but she didn't feel right either. She felt uneasy and it was unsettling. She got a spiral notebook and stretched out across the bed.

I feel like I'm at a crossroads. I feel like I'm too young to have accomplished anything substantial, but I also feel too old to not have initiated something meaningful. I don't know how to

Keleya stopped. 'Why am I doing this?' she thought. She hadn't kept a journal since age ten. Keleya read what she'd written. She wasn't feeling the method, so she tore the page out and balled it up. She proceeded to do what she should have done in the first place. Just as Keleya was about to attach posts to a pair of yellow, pink and green thread earrings, her phone rang. She reached over to place the call on speaker and said, "What is it?"

"Thanks for takin Nya over Momma's house yesterday," Nkosazana said.

"Mmm hmm."

"What's wrong with you?"

"What you think?"

Nkosazana exhaled deeply in the phone. "Why you always throwin me shade?"

"What the hell did you expect when you called? You expected me to be giddy or somethin?" Nkosazana didn't respond. "That wasn't a rhetorical question."

"Look, I don't feel like hearin this right now. I'll talk to you later."

"Zana you called me, so I think you can talk for a minute… why you lie to me yesterday?"

"Who said I was lyin?"

"You knew I was bringin Janya home around 6:00, so I don't understand why—"

"Leya what's the problem! She went over Momma's house. Damn!"

"Zana that's not the mutha-fuckin-point! You lied to me with my niece sittin there listenin to everything I was sayin and then I had to turn around and lie to her cause of you. And I guess nevermind what Janya might be thinkin cause obviously this dude that you was laid up with must be so good you couldn't tear yourself away to get your child. Shit, Janya may be five, but she ain't dumb."

"Who said I was with a man?"

"Girl…I know you better than you know yourself if you gone ask me that dumb ass question. You'd fuck anything."

"Keleya why the hell you always runnin your mouth like you know every goddamn thing? In case you forgot, I'm grown! Do I say anything to you about what you be doing?"

"Doing?"

"Did you not fuck Kris last night? Did she not cheat on you? Did she not tear your shit up?" Nkosazana questioned. Keleya paused and the argument died. She became fixated on understanding…guessing how her sister knew about the prior night with Kris. "I came by your apartment this morning to talk to you," Nkosazana continued. "But I saw her car outside. What? Did Kris leave and come back this morning? You sayin I can't get mine too?"

Keleya was sure that no one would ever know about *that*, but it was now clear that Kris had left too late. And now, less than twenty-four hours later, her secret was out and in the wrong mouth. So in her defense, Keleya slowly said, "N—ko—sa—zana, I *know* you ain't comparing me being with *my ex*—who I spent four years of my life with—to *you* and *your* promiscuity." Nkosazana was silent. "I mean for real," Keleya continued. "I know you not comparing my four year commitment to your four minute fucks." *Click.* "Hello?" Keleya proceeded to immediately call Nkosazana back, but her restraint suddenly kicked in. She placed her cell phone on the table. The quarrel was over.

In retrospect, I realized that everything that I wanted to say about that situation was said. So I'm content. If Nkosazana has anything else to say, she can call me.

April 23rd

KELEYA LEFT WORK and headed to her mother's house to visit Stacy, Jayden and Jayla. They didn't visit the previous month, so Stacy decided they would stay the entire weekend. Keleya hadn't talked to Nkosazana since their argument on Sunday, so she wasn't sure if she would be there too. When she pulled into the yard, Keleya didn't see Stacy's car. She walked into the house, door unlocked as normal, to see Rita and the children in the den. "Momma, why the door not locked?" Keleya asked, awaiting her response.

"Cause Stacy is at Easy Way getting some greens. She'll be right back."

"Okay, but one of them can easily unlock the door when she gets back."

"She won't be gone long," Rita replied. About five minutes later, Stacy arrived with twelve bunches of turnips for Rita to cook. As usual, Rita went into the kitchen while Keleya stayed in the den playing with Jayden and Jayla.

Keleya sat on the floor wondering why Janya was not with her cousins. She talked to her niece a few times during the week, but she was still tempted to ask her mother if she'd heard from Nkosazana. On second thought, she didn't want to open up that can of worms with Rita. Besides, Nkosazana always pulled the I-won't-let-my-child-come-around-act whenever she was mad with anyone in the family—often using Janya as bait to gain attention and sympathy while being distant.

"Keleya!" Rita screamed. "Come in here for a minute." Before walking into the kitchen, Keleya pulled a freezer bag full of jewelry from her purse. When she entered the kitchen, Rita asked, "How come you and your sister ain't talkin?"

"What do you mean? I am talkin to Stacy," Keleya responded in an attempt to slow the dialogue that would soon unfold.

Rita ignored her daughter's deliberate avoidance. "Why y'all mad at each other?"

"She ain't already told you?" Keleya asked. 'Shit, that's a shock,' Keleya thought.

"I'm askin you, right?" Rita replied. "Sit down." Rita and Stacy were sitting in their usual places. However, Rita sat at the table to get clarification. Stacy sat to be nosey. And Keleya sat to be respectful. "Well?" Rita said sternly.

Keleya exhaled, placed the bag of necklaces and bracelets on the table and coiled a tress of her two-strand twist-out around a finger. "Momma, you makin this more than what it is. It ain't that big of a deal."

"That's for me to decide," Rita responded. Keleya still didn't have anything to say because she was not in the mood to rerun the incident. "Keleya, don't make me call your sister. Now either you gone tell me or I'm gone get it out the other horse's mouth." Keleya was still silent. "Stacy, slide that phone over here." Stacy followed her mother's command and propelled the cordless phone across the glass top table, but Keleya intercepted. "Give me the phone," Rita demanded.

"No."

"Keleya Rochelle Smith don't play with me!"

"Momma. Why? No." Rita stood to seize the phone from

her daughter's hands. Keleya began to laugh so hard that she could no longer keep a grip. Rita snatched the phone away and sat down to dial Nkosazana's number, but Keleya conceded. "Okay…dog!"

"What happened?" Rita asked with zero tolerance in her voice.

"Zana mad cause I roasted her ass…roasted her about what happened Saturday?"

"You mean when Janya came over here?"

"Yeah. She was supposed to be at home so I could drop Nya off, but when I called she didn't wanna get her. So she asked me to bring Nya over here."

"And what's wrong with that?"

"Momma, you don't put your child off on somebody else just so you can spend time with some man. Now I know you didn't have a problem with your grandchild comin over here, but I do have a problem with Zana lyin to me."

"How you know she was with somebody?" Rita asked. Keleya couldn't even dignify that question with a response. So she looked at her mother with a you-do-know-who-we're-talking-about look on her face. "If your sister needed you to keep Janya for a little while, what's the problem?"

'You always defending her!' Keleya thought. "The problem is that if you tell somebody somethin, you don't turn around and renege on what you said just because you happen to be inconvenienced, and you shole don't do it when your child is involved," Keleya said annoyed.

"So that's what y'all argued about?" Rita asked.

"No, we argued about the fact that your daughter's a hoe," Keleya said boldly.

"Ooh," Stacy crooned as Rita simultaneously said, "Excuse me Keleya?"

"Momma I'm sorry, but ain't no need to be pretty with it."

To relieve the tension, Stacy decided to deposit her two cents. "Well look, that is not what Zana told me."

"What?" Keleya asked. "So you told Momma about this?"

"Does it matter?" Stacy questioned.

"Of course it does! If you done already talked to Zana why you sittin in front of Momma actin like you don't know what happened, askin me to give a run down?"

"All I know is that Zana felt judged. She felt that the only reason you reacted the way you did is because you wanted to spend time with Kris, not Janya."

"Hold up!" Keleya said with a chuckle. She was flabbergasted. "Why would I accuse Zana of somethin and then turn around do it myself? And you got the game wrong if you think I was tryin to get rid of Janya just so I could be with Kris. At the end of the day, Zana was wrong, I told her the way I felt about the situation and she bets not do it again to me or Janya."

Rita listened quietly. But by this time, she'd heard enough and was ready to change the subject. "So you and your friend together again?"

"My *girl*friend?" Keleya said to correct her mother. "No." Keleya suddenly wondered if Nkosazana had told Stacy about her little "incident."

"You seein anybody?" Rita continued.

"No ma'am," Keleya answered. After everything that was just said, she felt no reason to tell her mother or sister about her date with Jordan the following day. "Why you ask me that?"

"I'm just askin...you lookin for somebody?"

"No." Keleya felt the questioning was strange so she asked, "What are you tryin to ask me?"

"Why you think I got somethin up my sleeve?"

"Because you actin weird."

"I know right," Stacy added.

Rita laughed. "No…sometimes I look at my girls and I can't believe ya'll are women. It's just too much for me sometimes."

"Momma, don't get sentimental," Stacy said.

"Hush!" Rita snapped. Keleya thought her reaction was hell of funny so she burst into laughter. Doing so made the three of them relax a bit and finally start to enjoy each other's company. They sat in the kitchen together as Rita cooked turnip greens, cornbread, baked pork chops and sweet tea. As the food simmered, Rita and Stacy went through the bag of jewelry, admiring Keleya's craftsmanship and divvying the pieces they fancied. After eating, they took the kids in the backyard to play.

I didn't appreciate the fact that Stacy put my argument with Zana on blast to Momma. But in the end, the fact that Momma knew wasn't a big a deal. Once I let go of that I had a good time, mainly because I allowed myself to do something I had not done in a very long time— I talked to my sister.

April 24th

KELEYA WAS SO preoccupied during the week that she didn't realize how much she looked forward to seeing and talking to Jordan again. She was anxious, but slightly embarrassed by the anticipation. She heard a car pulling in outside, so she got up to peer through the blinds and divert attention away from how she felt. There was someone visiting an upstairs neighbor. Just before Keleya moved from the window, she saw Kris' car drive by. Surprising! The only other person they both knew in the apartment complex was Soria. Keleya knew that Kris had purposefully driven past because you didn't have to go by her apartment to get to where Soria lived.

Keleya first saw Soria while walking around the neighborhood one day. She saw a Black woman around her age kiss another similarly aged woman goodbye. She looked in Keleya's direction and spoke. A couple days later, Keleya and Kris were walking together and saw the same young woman outside, this time alone. Keleya and Kris became acquainted with Soria, but Kris never knew her well enough to warrant private visits. Or so she thought.

Keleya did not want to be retaliatory with her emotions, but she was now undeniably excited about the prospect of getting to know someone new. She asked Jordan to meet her at Walton Park at 6:00 because it would be awkward if Jordan came to the apartment. Jordan asked Keleya to plan the evening, so Keleya chose two things she enjoyed—the park and food. Keleya wanted to get there first to feel more settled. After all, she hadn't talked to or dated another woman in years. But when she got out the car and walked towards the bench, she saw a figure that she partially recognized. "What's up?" Jordan greeted.

"Hey," Keleya said while continuing to walk towards her. "Did you have trouble finding this place?"

"Sort of," Jordan responded as they both sat down. "What's on the agenda for today?" Before answering, Keleya smiled and looked away. "What?" Jordan asked.

"Nothing," Keleya replied, ogling. "I just...you're very attractive," Keleya stated. Jordan laughed. Keleya looked at Jordan from head to toe and noticed a small, Chinese lettered tattoo below her right thumb. And the yellow polo shirt was the perfect compliment to her beautiful brown skin. The jeans... the Tims...she looked *nice*. A thin brown headband bound Jordan's wavy, semi-kinky hair. Some Black folks foolishly called this texture "good hair." Growing up, Rita called it "soft hair." Either way, Keleya had never been too keen to it and felt it looked strange as locs. Nevertheless, what Keleya really found appealing about Jordan was the persona. Jordan seemed completely comfortable and confident in herself. Her femininity was paired with a dash of masculinity, but she didn't seem to perform her gender. It was a natural expression and Keleya *liked* it. "You are easy on the eyes," she continued. Jordan blushed. Keleya wasn't the type to overtly or boldly flirt. But given what occurred earlier that day, she didn't mind putting her feelings out there.

"Thanks. You are too," Jordan replied while glancing at Keleya's cleavage.

"Have you been to Rico's Wings?" Keleya asked to move past sensual thoughts. Jordan shook her head and said no. "I figured we would go there first. It's a mom and pop in Frayser."

"Is that were you're from?"

"Yeah. You've been here for a while so I'm sure you've been to Frayser, right?"

"Yeah, two of my clients' families live in Frayser."

"Well, they say you haven't experienced a place until you've eaten there."

Jordan smiled. "What's so special about Rico's?"

"Nice folks, good food, Black owned. And it's in my old stompin ground. That's it."

"And what's after that?"

"I don't know. We can find somethin to get into."

"Cool."

After getting in Keleya's Maxima and heading to their first destination, Jordan asked about her workweek. "It was a'ight," Keleya replied.

"Why just a'ight?"

"Because I can't stand folks and their egos. And I can't stand people who are hell bent on their job title…plus, I'm one of a few at that place."

"You mean Black or female? Or both?"

"Black in particular. But really, the issue is that some people I work with expect me to be a certain way or open to certain activities because I went to college…or just because I work there I guess. But I do my job and I do it well and that's all that should matter…what about you?"

"Honestly, I'm gettin to the point where I'm havin to recalibrate the balance between my emotions and my professionalism. Some stuff is really gettin under my skin."

"Like what? If you don't mind answering."

"Where do I begin? Well…I work mostly with African

American youth and families—of course this is Memphis—but I've never been in an environment where nobody can take accountability for their actions and how it affects their children. I ain't saying it wasn't the same way in Philly. It's just a barefaced fact in this city. Now, I consider myself to be a fairly intelligent woman so I've tried to come up with some answers. I'm like is it the school system? The culture? A breakdown in the family? A lack of pride? Or…hell I don't know. I just hate the fact that Black people are so damn ignorant and disconnected."

"Yes ma'am…I hear you." Keleya could see through her peripheral vision that Jordan was looking at her. So she looked at Jordan after a few seconds. When she did so, Jordan smiled. "What are you smilin about?"

Jordan flashed her lovely smile again and scanned her eyes along Keleya's body. "Right now, some things are best left in the imagination."

"You gettin fresh with me Ms. Alexander?"

"Very much so," Jordan replied. Keleya laughed. "You're beautiful…and you made me wait weeks to see you again."

"Weeks? It has not been that long."

"Hell, I should know. You shot me down last week."

Keleya laughed. "Right."

"You ain't got nothin to say about the beautiful part?" Jordan asked.

"No. That's your judgment call, not mine."

Jordan laughed. "You don't like compliments?"

"No, not really."

"So no flattery?"

"I don't prefer it."

"Are you serious?"

"Very much so," Keleya replied.

Jordan laughed and leaned closer to Keleya. "Would you prefer me to show you rather than tell you?"

"Don't get crafty with me," Keleya smiled. The obvious and strong attraction was becoming overwhelming. Fortunately, Keleya was able to change the subject. "That's Rico's to the right, on the corner."

"I drove past here once. Didn't notice it though." Once inside, Keleya and Jordan ordered wing combos and sat in a booth by the window. "You plan to eat all that," Jordan asked.

"I don't eat like this often. So yes."

"Most women I know wouldn't throw down like that on the first date. They'd be too busy worrying about lookin pretty."

"Date? It that what this is?" Keleya joked. "I like to eat. Plus, I'm not worried about being pretty or gaining weight. I'm just tryin to maintain it."

"Yeah, you did tell me you run on a regular basis," Jordan commented. She was hesitant to ask the following question, but she couldn't resist. "So…you used to be bigger?"

"Bigger? Is that an alternative for fat? You got a problem with big girls?" Keleya asked smiling.

"No…I'm just asking."

"I've had to shed some pounds that I packed on during undergrad."

"That's normal. I had some friends who did too."

"You keep in touch with any of them?"

"Not really. I talk to an ex sometimes, but that's it."

"You went to school together?"

"Yeah, but we didn't graduate together because I was always on the grind and she was always in the scene. That's one of the main reasons we didn't work out." Keleya shook her head in understanding, but her attention was diverted to a female patron entering the restaurant. Her name was Shalonda and she waved at Keleya. Keleya was courteous enough to give a quick, half wave back. "You know her?"

"*Used* to know her," Keleya replied.

"Do I sense some bad blood there?"

Keleya responded with a half–truth. "No. We used to be tight. Then we went our separate ways." The whole truth was that Keleya and Shalonda were each other's firsts. "And that's why I don't like comin out here cause I always see somebody I know…or knew."

"Seemed like some animosity was there because of the way you acknowledged her."

Keleya laughed. "You would have got a different reaction out of me if that was the case."

"How far from here did you grow up?"

"I lived in three different places around here, but what I consider home is about five minutes that way," Keleya said as she motioned to the west.

"That's where you lived when you left Memphis?"

"Yeah."

"You ever go back to visit?"

"Yeah," Keleya said puzzled. "My momma lives there," she clarified.

"Ooh. I've been under the impression that your family no longer lived out here…or maybe I just assumed it."

"No, she's still there."

"Okay, okay. So has Frayser always been like this?"

"Like what? You mean a lil hood?"

Jordan smiled. "Yeah, in so many words."

"No, it's changed over the years."

"You plan to stay in Memphis?"

"Oh no. I definitely wanna leave. I can see myself stayin here for a few more years, but after that I'm jettin."

"To where?"

"I don't know yet…you plan on going back to Philadelphia?"

"Maybe. But *I am* leaving Memphis."

"Why?" Keleya asked. "Us country folk too slow for you?"

"Hell yeah," Jordan laughed. "Naw, but for real, I gotta be somewhere with mass transit. And I wanna be somewhere more liberal. I mean damn. Can ya'll work on getting some gay rights in this city…a Hetrick Martin or somethin."

"Hetrick Martin? Girl please! They don't even have one of those in Philly. The only thing that would make folks round here get off they asses would be if Colored Only/White Only signs reappeared. Most folks round here got they heads so far in the Bible they'd miss the second coming." Jordan laughed. "Looks like you *will* be leavin Memphis," Keleya stated.

"You can come with me," Jordan said in her sexy voice. Keleya had talked to her long enough to now recognize it.

"You gettin fresh with me again Ms. Alexander?"

Jordan smiled. "What's up with the word fresh? You sound like somebody's momma."

"I know. My momma says it all the time."

The conversation continued for the next hour. Keleya found Jordan easy to talk to. The more they talked, the more Keleya learned about the things they had in common despite the fact that they'd grown up in two completely different cities and families. As it turns out, Jordan grew up in a six-figure household. Jordan's mother, a Political Science professor, and father, CEO of a large nonprofit, were second-generation college students who met in college. Jordan followed in her father's footsteps by majoring in Social Work. Although separated by distance, her parents were still married and very much in love. Jordan learned that Keleya's mother built a career in Human Resources by garnering work experience and that Keleya was the first generation college student in her immediate family. When they got in the car, Jordan asked about her father.

"I don't know exactly what he does," Keleya explained. "Last I heard he worked for the City of Little Rock."

"The two of you don't talk often?" Jordan asked.

"He calls sometimes."

"You got other siblings?"

"As far as I know, I'm his only child. But the woman he married has two sons."

"So he's not your sisters' father?"

"Nope. We have different donors," Keleya answered. That was the end of that topic. Ten minutes later, Keleya spotted an ice cream shop. "You wanna stop over there?"

"Yeah, that's cool," Jordan replied. Just as they were pulling into the parking lot, the subject turned to similarities again. "So why didn't you join a sorority? You seem like one of them Delta types to me."

"What? I feel like people go Greek for two reasons: they're legacy or they have low self-esteem. And I didn't fit the bill for either one." Jordan held the door open for Keleya as they stepped into the shop. Once in line Keleya asked, "What would you like?"

Jordan continued to look at the menu. "I don't know... they got a lot of stuff."

"Yeah they do." Jordan took a few more seconds to look at the menu. After telling Keleya what she wanted, Jordan moved out of line to stand behind the divider while waiting.

"Can I help you?" asked the White, middle-aged cashier in a heavy country accent. Her nametag read "Linda."

"Can I get a medium Oreo milkshake and a medium cup of strawberry ice cream?"

"Okay...would you like anything else?" Linda asked.

"No ma'am. That's it," Keleya answered.

"Will that be for here or to go?"

"For here?" Keleya said, but she was confused by the question. She didn't think an ice cream order warranted a for-here-or-to-go option. She stepped out of line and stood by Jordan.

"What did she ask you?" Jordan asked.

"If the order was for here or to go."

"I didn't know people asked that at ice cream joints."

"Hell, me neither," Keleya commented.

Two minutes later, Keleya went back to the counter to pick up the order. As Linda slid the two containers across the counter she said in a low voice, "I just wanna say this a family environment, but it's okay for you to stay this time."

Keleya was hell of confused now. Her initial reaction was to look back. So she looked in Jordan's direction and thought, 'Did she say that because we're Black?' But that didn't make sense because there were several African American customers in the shop. So she moved to her second reaction. "What did you just say?"

"There are kids in here and we prefer not to have homosexuality in front of them," Linda added. At this point, Keleya was shocked. 'Homosexuality in front of them,' she thought. The wording was so idiomatic that Keleya sort of laughed. "I'm not trying to make a scene," Linda continued. "I tried to say it as respectful as I could." Keleya was now a split second away from picking up one of the containers and throwing it in her damn face, but she didn't want to get hood the first time out with Jordan. She bit her tongue and walked away.

"What's going on?" Jordan asked.

"She just told me that they don't want homosexuals in here."

"What? Are you serious?"

"Yes," Keleya said before walking to the exit. Once outside and at the car, Keleya realized Jordan was still inside. She leaned against the car door to wait. Jordan walked out less than a minute later. "What did she say to you?"

"Nothing. I told her not to say shit to me and to give me a refund," Jordan replied as she handed Keleya the money. "Why did you walk out?"

"The best thing for me to do was walk away."

"I can't believe that shit. That's why I gotta get..." Jordan continued to vent, but Keleya didn't listen. Instead, she stood with her arms crossed, peering at the ground while replaying the last ten minutes in her head. 'We pulled up, got out the car, went in, stood in line...' "What exactly did she say?" Jordan asked, prompting Keleya to redirect her attention.

"That she didn't want homosexuality in front of the kids."

"What?"

"That's what she said."

"So she assumed we were together."

Keleya shook her head yes as she moved to open the car door. After turning the ignition and putting the gear in reverse, Keleya continued. "She must have seen you hold the door for me. Then she looked at you and assumed that we were homo—sex–u–als," Keleya said, mimicking Linda's Southern drawl. Keleya hoped her statement didn't offend Jordan, but it was fact.

"Yeah," Jordan said softly as she thought about the incident. "What do you wanna do now? You wanna to call it a night?"

"No...I'm not lettin that shit get to me. You decide."

Jordan suggested that we go to a bar that she'd been to a few times with coworkers, Angie included. Upon entering the bar, I reminded myself that a few drinks would not turn into anything more and that I would be going home alone...not that sexing it up on the first date is in my nature, it just seemed like the right thing to do. After several hours of good convo and laughs, we left at 1:00. And despite the homophobic misfortune we experienced that evening, I enjoyed every moment that night.

April 28th

ALMOST FOUR DAYS had passed since Keleya's date with Jordan and she looked forward to seeing her again. So when Jordan offered to come by her apartment after work, Keleya didn't hesitate in texting back yes.

What's your address?
2074 Rivercross. What time you get off?
7. I'll call u when I leave.
K.

Keleya left work at her usual time. She went home, changed clothes and went to the park to work out. After a forty-five minute jog, she returned home and took a shower. Jordan called thirty minutes later to say she was on the way. When Keleya heard her SUV pull up outside, she opened the door and walked onto the porch. Jordan stepped out of the truck and set the alarm. "Hey," she said as she walked toward Keleya.

"Hey come in."

"You live closer than I thought."

"I told you it wasn't far from your job...have a seat," Keleya said as she locked the door.

Jordan sat on the corner of the chaise lounge. "You got a nice place."

"Thanks."

"I wanted to look in this area when I started to look for a place to live, but my mom wanted me live near to her and my grandma."

"Where exactly do you live?"

"Off Mendenhall near Poplar."

Keleya shook her head okay. "Why did you get your own apartment? You didn't want to live with them?"

"Man, I haven't lived with my momma since I was eighteen. And the one month I stayed with them was long enough."

"You couldn't pay me to live in my momma's house again," Keleya commented. "You want somethin to drink?"

"Yeah, thanks. What do you have?" Jordan asked.

"Hmm...honestly I don't know." Keleya got up and walked to the refrigerator to list beverages. After handing Jordan a Coke, she sat beside her. "You just left work, you hungry? You want me to make you somethin to eat?"

"Like what?"

"What do you like?"

"What can you cook?"

"Anything. Tell me what you want. If I have it I'll make it."

"I don't know...I don't wanna go home sick."

Keleya laughed. "How you gone come over here and insult me? Woman, I can cook...you like spaghetti?"

"Yeah."

"You eat green beans?"

"Yeah."

"Okay, I'll cook you dinner."

"Are you for real? You're gonna cook for me right now?"

"Yeah!" Keleya said as she stood from the couch. "That's what I said." She stood in front of Jordan and held out her

ACCEPT THE UNEXPECTED

hand as an official invitation. Jordan took Keleya's hand and
was led to a bar stool at the kitchen island. She took a seat
and talked to Keleya while she made spaghetti, green beans
and fried chicken drumettes, complemented with Cole's garlic
bread. Less than an hour later, Keleya sat two full plates on the
island countertop and walked to the opposite side to sit on the
stool next to Jordan.

"Wow," Jordan commented. "This looks good...thanks
Keleya. I appreciate it."

"You're welcome. And the meat is thoroughly cooked. I
promise."

After finishing dinner, Keleya and Jordan returned to the
sectional. "Oh my god I'm full," Jordan said as she leaned
back. "That was good. I ain't had food that good in months."

"Does your mother cook for you?" Keleya asked.

"No. She can't cook to save her life. My grandmother can,
but since I've been here she's only threw down once. And that
was when we first moved here...can I come back tomorrow?"

"Yes you can...anytime."

Jordan smiled and said, "I'm serious."

"I am too."

"Okay...what you doing Friday?"

"Nothing," Keleya replied. "I'll be with you." Jordan
laughed. "You can come over or we'll go out...or both."

*I knew at some point Jordan would ask about the mask. I dreaded
it, but I knew it was coming. I gave her a minimal explanation and
changed the subject. We continued to talk and around 10:30 Jordan went
home. When she left, I put the spaghetti away and placed the dishes in
the dishwasher. I went in my room and got in the bed to relax and read a
book. But I didn't read it...I couldn't. Instead, I listened to the TV and
thought about Jordan...I really like her. And I'm surprised about it...I
didn't know that I could have feelings for another woman so soon.*

June 11th

POST THEIR FIRST date, Keleya and Jordan communicated daily through emails at work or talks in the evening. In doing so, Keleya's schedule acquired a new routine: all free time was reserved for Jordan. Conversations grew intimate as acquaintanceship bud mutual affection, which ripened a shared and tender emotion. Keleya was not prepared for the long haul of commitment, but stood open to the possibilities of romance and companionship. As she was preparing for the evening with Jordan, JaCola called. "Leya, can you text me Zana's number?" JaCola asked, no greeting.

"Yeah," Keleya replied.

"She still got them purses?"

"I don't know."

"I'll call her later and see."

"You at work?" Keleya asked.

"Shit yeah. I don't get off til midnight. What you doing?'

"About to go to Jordan's apartment and to the movies."

"I thought you'd never been to her apartment?"

"I hadn't…until last week."

"Umm! Well…have fun."

"Uh! Why you gotta say it like that?"

"Cause…I'm just a little surprised."

"Why?"

"We can talk about that later cause I gotta go."

Keleya sent a text with her sister's phone number while thinking about the short conversation. She was bothered by JaCola's reaction, but pushed that aside and continued to dress. Once at Jordan's apartment, there was time to spare so they waited a while before leaving. As Keleya sat on the love seat flipping through the channels, something made her glance at the end table. She looked over and saw a five-pack of Black and Mild and two Swisher Sweets. Jordan re-entered the living room a few seconds later. She paused to type and send a text before sitting. "You smoke Blacks?" Keleya asked.

"Hmm?" Jordan responded. She looked down and noticed the cigars. "No." Jordan grabbed the cigars and placed them in the cabinet of the entertainment center.

"Then…what?" Keleya inquired. After thinking about it for a second, she asked, "You smoke weed?" Jordan sat beside Keleya and stared at the wall. "Are you going to answer me?"

Jordan sat back and looked at Keleya. "Yeah."

"How is that possible?"

"Trust me, it's possible," Jordan replied.

Keleya could tell by Jordan's blank expression that she was uncomfortable. However, she didn't care. "So…why do you get high and how high do you get?" Keleya prodded.

Jordan laughed to relieve apprehension of the ensuing conversation. "It's part of my self-care management," she joked.

"Really? What level of management are you talking about?"

"Weekly management."

"You mean on the weekends? Weekdays? What?"

"It depends."

"It depends on what?"

"Stress levels."

"Can you stop givin me one and two word answers?"

Jordan exhaled. She leaned back and looked at the ceiling. "When I was twenty-four my brother was in a real bad motorcycle accident and was in a coma for a minute. I was in grad school full-time and it was...too much. At the time, I was dating this girl who smoked from sun up to sun down...and I started doing it too...not like her...but it became my coping mechanism."

"What is it now?"

"It's...it's still a stress reliever. Shit, I don't know."

"Do people in your family know?" Keleya asked.

"Just my brother and my cousin Tranesha...smoking weed is not somethin that's supposed to be associated with what I do." She looked at Keleya and asked, "Do you have a problem with this?"

"No, I don't...I say do what you do, just know why you're doing it." After that statement, Keleya left the matter alone. They left in Jordan's SUV and went to the movies. Two hours and fifteen minutes later, they exited the theater. "Did you like movie?" Keleya asked.

"No. Not really...did you?"

"Uh uhh. It could've been better."

"What do you wanna do? You wanna get somethin to eat?" Jordan asked. Then she smiled. "I know you wanna go back to that restaurant."

"Ooh, don't even mention it. The food was good as hell, but I don't need to eat like that again."

"If you wanna go, let's go...just don't order so much?"

"What? What you tryin to say?" Keleya smiled. "That I ate too much or that I spent too much of your money?"

Jordan laughed and unlocked the doors. "You're the one who said somethin about it. Shit, you know you can eat."

Before leaving the parking space, Jordan checked her texts. "Angie just text me. She said she's at Hard Rock on Beale if we wanna come by."

"You must have told her we'd be together tonight?"

"Yeah...at work yesterday. Somethin wrong with that?"

"No, I was just asking."

"So do you wanna go?"

"Yeah that's fine." Keleya and Jordan joined Angie at a table near the bar. After speaking and sitting, Angie introduced Keleya to Renée. And after greeting Renée, Keleya asked, "So the three of you work together?"

"Yeah," Angie responded.

"Okay. It's nice to meet you Renée."

"You too," Renée responded. Keleya noticed that after the introduction, Renée continued to look at her. And every time Keleya looked in her direction, Renée would avert her gaze. Keleya wasn't sure if the stares were because she'd intruded on their coworker, buddy–buddy time or if Renée just couldn't control it. Either way, Renée was making her uncomfortable as hell. Then she noticed that Renée was actually monitoring her verbal and physical interaction with Jordan. Nonetheless, Keleya continued to act as if she was not disturbed by the constant observation.

After forty minutes of conversation, Jordan and Renée entered into a discussion about Southern living. Renée was a former Philadelphian who never wanted to live in the northeast again, whereas Jordan was a die-hard Philly girl. And given that neither Keleya nor Angie could identify, they turned their attention to each other. "Why you lookin at me like that Angie?" Keleya asked.

"I'm good right?" Angie asked in return.

"Good at what?"

"With hookin folks up. I knew ya'll would like each

other…I should be paid," Angie bragged.

"Paid for what?"

"Hell, a successful match."

Keleya laughed and rolled her eyes. "So what's up with the two of you?" she asked, referencing Renée with her eyes.

"Nothin. We work together."

"Work *and* play together?"

Angie smiled and took a sip of Coke and Hennessey. "It ain't like that. We're just friends."

Keleya wanted to comment about Renée's odd infatuation, but she refrained. "Why? You don't like her? She looks like yo type Angie."

"And what's that?"

Keleya glanced at Renée and figured she was at least thirty-four or thirty-five years of age. "A cute, petite, weaved up older woman."

"Yeah, you got me pegged," Angie laughed. "But we're friends. That's it…what's up with ya'll?"

Keleya stared at Angie for a few seconds. "Why you askin me a question you already know the answer to?"

"What? Keleya I wouldn't have asked you if I knew what was up. And why you think we be at working tellin each other all our business? It ain't like that. If you don't wanna tell me, I'll ask Jordan to—"

"Ask me what?" Jordan interjected.

"What's up with ya'll?" Angie continued.

"Us?" Jordan asked as she gestured between herself and Keleya. "Ask her." Jordan looked at Keleya and asked, "What's up with us? Cause I don't know. Tell me."

Keleya smiled for a second. "We are…I don't know. What would you call it?"

"We're asking you," Jordan replied.

"Are you dating?" Renée asked. "Because if you are, that's a start."

"Thank you," Keleya replied. "Yes, you can call it dating."

"What do mean you can call it dating?" Angie questioned. "Either you is or you ain't."

"Look! We got this. It is what it is," Keleya stated.

"Ya'll still young. You got time to figure it out," Angie stated as if she were significantly older than both Keleya and Jordan, but she was only thirty-one.

A few minutes later, Angie and Renée excused themselves and went to the restroom while Keleya and Jordan continued to talk. "What you doing tomorrow?" Jordan asked.

"My grandma came in today, so I'm going to spend some time with her."

"Yeah, that's right. You did tell me that...so...I guess I won't see you tomorrow."

"No you can...I'll call you when I leave," Keleya said, but Jordan didn't reply. "You're lookin at me like I'm lyin or somethin."

"No...I was thinkin about how good you look tonight," Jordan commented as she rubbed her fingers across the black, beaded necklace Keleya wore before resting her hand on the broad belt around Keleya's waist. "I wanna kiss you," she said softly. Keleya blushed. The feeling was mutual and her desire to cross personal spaces was definitely ablaze. But Keleya was not a fan of PDA. Plus, they were sitting in the midst of a bustling establishment. "You don't wanna kiss me?" Jordan asked as she rubbed Keleya's hand.

"I do...it's just..."

"What?"

"I don't want you to get the impression that I'm ashamed because that's not the case. But this is not Philadelphia Jordan."

"Philadelphia?" Jordan questioned. "Keleya the situation wouldn't be any different if we were in Philly." Before Jordan could continue, Angie and Renée returned, turning the "situation" into an ill at ease one. "Look, you don't have to now, but you will when we leave."

And she was right. When they approached the car, Jordan opened the door for Keleya. Then she took Keleya's hand and pulled her close. Jordan looked Keleya in her eyes and kissed her without hesitation…and it felt too right. It felt good enough to undress, so Keleya slowly pulled away and got in the car. As Jordan walked to the driver's side, Keleya took a deep breath. But she couldn't control her feelings. When Jordan got in the car and looked at Keleya, she was irresistible. So Keleya pulled her close again and kissed her intensely. Jordan placed her hand on Keleya's inner thigh, waiting for a go. But Keleya stopped. She couldn't start something that she wouldn't finish.

As they rode back to the apartment, Keleya tamed herself by squeezing her legs together a couple of times. She figured some stimulation was better than none at all. Once at the apartment, they sat in the car for a while and talked. When they got out, Keleya forced herself to walk to her car and not inside Jordan's apartment. Jordan walked with her to say goodbye and they kissed each other goodnight. "Are you sure you wanna leave?" Jordan asked as she kissed Keleya's neck.

Keleya smiled and said, "Please don't."

"Call me when you get home tomorrow," Jordan said as she let her go.

"I will."

I definitely will!

June 12th

KELEYA FLIPPED THROUGH a hair and lifestyle magazine to pass time as she underwent a deep hair conditioning. She was becoming hot and irritable, so she tossed the magazine back onto the table. She had no patience for the beauty shop ritual. Fortunately, her ringing phone was a temporary distraction. "What's up?" Keleya answered.

"Where you?" Nkosazana asked.

"At the beauty shop."

"How long you been there?"

"Not long. I'm under the dryer."

"Umm, you still got some time to go then."

"Tasha don't take that long to do hair, so I should be out of here in an hour. She know I gots to be in and out."

"You comin over here when you leave?"

"Yeah."

"Alright, I'll see you when you get here."

After ending the call, Keleya thought about calling her sister back. But she decided to practice a little patience until Tasha relieved her from the dryer. Eight minutes later, Tasha directed Keleya to her chair. "Thank God," Keleya exclaimed as she lifted the dryer.

"Girl...sit down. You wasn't even under there long. It's only been fifteen minutes," Tasha pointed out.

"That's too long for me. I don't know why you just can't blow dry my hair like I asked you to."

"Look! I done told you once and I'm gone tell you again. You not comin to my shop without sittin under the dryer. So stop tryin to tell me how to do my job," Tasha said as she pushed Keleya's head forward to run the hand-held blow dryer through the back of her hair. "How you want me to style your hair?"

"Just trim it and press it. And can you use the comb too cause I don't like the way it feels with just a flat iron?"

"Yeah...what you been up to?" Tasha asked.

"Nothin. You know ain't nothin to do around here. How you been?"

"Good girl," Tasha said while smacking on a piece of hard candy. "I'm tryin to get my boys ready for school."

"School? They startin school this year?"

"Yep. They start kindergarten in September. Janya's going to first grade, right?"

"Mmm hmm. And I can't believe it. My baby is gettin old."

"I saw her and Zana the other day at the store," Tasha recalled.

"For real? Was it just them?"

"Girl stop," Tasha laughed. "I know you ain't tryin to talk about my friend," she said to defend her high school classmate. "You plan on seein her today?"

"Yeah."

"Remind me to give you this money before you leave. I got her down for some time next week, but I need to give it to her before I forget."

"Okay." Keleya left the shop an hour later and headed for her mother's house. On her way there, her phone rang again.

She answered the long awaited call and said, "Hello."

"Hey Leya," Kris said in a manner that disregarded the fact they hadn't spoke in eight weeks.

"Hi."

"You busy?" Kris asked.

"No."

"You at home?"

"No. Why?"

"Have you received anything in the mail about my loans?"

"No, I don't think so. But I can look when I get back."

"Okay...how you doing?"

"I'm good...you?" Keleya asked lazily.

"I'm straight...do you not wanna talk to me?"

"Do you wanna talk to me?"

"Why you ask that?"

"Why the hell did you not return my calls?" Keleya asked as she pulled into her mother's driveway. "I guess you got what you wanted, right?"

Kris exhaled into the phone. "I know I'm wrong for not callin you back, but don't make it seem like I didn't have a reason not to. And don't make it seem like you didn't get shit in return."

"What do you mean a reason not to? Please explain boo."

"You think I don't know you talkin to somebody now? Shit...people talk Keleya."

"Kriston, you can make whatever excuse you want to for sleepin with me and then ignorin my calls, but don't worry. It won't happen again. I'll text you if I get your mail," Keleya said and ended the call. She stepped out of the car and walked into the house. She joined the family in the den and said hello to the children, who were sitting on the floor, and her sisters. She hugged her aunt, Tink, and her grandmother, Geraldine.

"Where you comin from? The beauty shop?" Geraldine

asked as Keleya sat beside her.

"Yes ma'am."

"Mmm hmm, I can smell it. Let me see your hair," Geraldine directed. Keleya turned her head. "It looks good."

"Thanks. What ya'll plan on doing today?" Keleya asked.

"I don't know. I gotta ask yo momma when she come back in here. She back there on the phone. But I think we posed to be going to Piccadilly."

'Eww. I hate Piccadilly,' Keleya thought. "Okay." She then asked about her younger cousin Shamar, Tink's grandson.

"He at home," Tink responded. "He couldn't come cause he had practice."

Keleya remembered the cash she was to give to Nkosazana. She took the $70 from her purse and handed it to her sister. "What's this for?" Nkosazana asked.

"It's from Tasha."

"Oh."

"What's the money for? A purse?" Keleya asked.

"Yeah."

"Where you gettin these purses from?"

"Don't worry about all that."

"Big Momma, ask her where she gettin these purses from. Cause she ain't gone lie to you."

"What purses?" Geraldine asked Keleya.

"Authentic brand name purses and wallets."

"Where you gettin them from?" Geraldine asked Nkosazana.

Nkosazana squinted at her sister, looked at her grandmother and said, "A friend." She then used her mother's entrance as an opportunity to change the subject. "Momma, we still going to Piccadilly?"

"Yeah," Rita responded. "Or we can go to Chili's or O'Charley's or somewhere. But tomorrow we cookin. And I should've went to Kroger yesterday, but I ain't have time to really do nothin."

"Momma, why didn't you say anything? I could have went this mornin," Stacy said.

"Cause I was busy!" Rita responded.

"What do you need?" Stacy asked. "I can go get it now."

"I don't know. I gotta write it down. Umm…Janya… go in the kitchen and get Granny that pen and paper off the table baby." Once she had the materials in hand, Rita wrote an extensive list and handed it to her daughter.

"Is this all?" Stacy asked sarcastically.

"Should be," Rita responded.

"Is anybody ridin with me?" Stacy asked as she grabbed her purse and stood.

"I'll go with you," Nkosazana stated and the children said they were going too. "No ya'll not! Ya'll stayin here." Jayda and Jayden waited for their mother to say otherwise, but she didn't.

"They comin right back," Rita commented. "As a matter of fact, ya'll need to go in the backyard." Rita stood to open the sliding door for her grandchildren. After their exit, she told her daughters to wait while she went to her bedroom to get cash for the groceries. She came back into the den and handed the money to Nkosazana. "And don't be all day."

After her sisters departed, Keleya talked with her grandmother and aunt. She learned that her grandmother was working part-time at the main library in her hometown. "I didn't know that," Keleya stated. "When did you start?"

"About a month ago," Geraldine replied. "Yo momma didn't tell you?"

"No ma'am she didn't."

"I thought I did," Rita said.

Keleya shook her head no. "What made you get a job?"

"I got tired of sittin at home. So Tink asked one of her

friends to let us know when somethin opened up. I don't do nothin but sit in the lobby and answer phones…and say hello to folks."

"She's a receptionist," Tink clarified.

"How many hours you workin?" Keleya asked.

"Four hours a day," Geraldine answered. "But I wanna work more."

"Momma you don't need no more hours," Rita asserted. "Twenty hours a week is enough." Rita and Geraldine spat back and forth about what was acceptable until Tink shared that Shamar would be employed part-time during the summer as well. Afterwards, Rita suggested that a decision be made about where the family would dine before Stacy and Nkosazana returned.

"It don't matter to me Rita," Geraldine stated.

"Me neither. You decide," Tink commented.

"You going with us Leya?" Rita asked.

"Yes. Why wouldn't I go Momma?"

"I figured you may wanna leave and go be with your friend since you don't spend time with your family no more," Rita explained.

"Momma, I'm over here all the time," Keleya remarked. "I always spend time with ya'll."

"You ain't been over here in weeks."

"That's because Stacy ain't came in weeks, not because of my new "friend" as you put it."

"What is she? Your girlfriend? Let me know so I can get it right."

"You with somebody else?" Tink asked. "What happened to the other one?"

'Other one?' Keleya thought. "We broke up months ago."

"Mmm!" Geraldine grunted loudly. "You going to church with us in the mornin?"

"No ma'am," Keleya replied. "But I'm comin over when ya'll get back."

"Why not? You *need* to go with us," Geraldine stated. 'Need?' Keleya thought. She loved her grandmother dearly, but she was not in the mood for proselytizing. "You don't believe in your Savior no more?"

"Momma, don't go there! Just leave it alone," Rita suggested. Keleya was relieved when her mother spoke in her defense. Surprisingly enough, Stacy and Nkosazana returned in reasonable time and Keleya was more than happy to help carry groceries inside the house. After everything was put in its proper place, the family went to Golden Corral.

Keleya got home a few minutes after 9:30. She sent Jordan a text and took a shower. When she got out the shower, there was no text from Jordan so she got dressed and called JaCola. Thirty minutes into their conversation, Jordan called. "Cola, hold on a minute," Keleya requested. She clicked over to talk to Jordan. "Hey."

"I just saw your text."

Keleya could hear the muddled sound of several voices and bass in the background. "Where are you?"

"At Tranesha's. You want company?"

"Yeah, but if you wanna stay you can call me tomorrow."

"Naw, I'm about to leave…but I need to go home first. I'll be there in about an hour."

"Alright." Keleya was about to end the call, but she remembered that JaCola was on hold. "Cola?"

"Yeah."

"Sorry, I know you don't like being on hold."

"Girl you good," JaCola stated. "I been screaming at Maleek anyway."

"Why?"

"Cause he won't stay in the bed. When he with his daddy,

he let him stay up all night. Now he don't wanna go to sleep."

"Let him lay with you. He'll fall asleep."

"He is! He layin right here beside me...close your eyes Maleek and go to sleep," JaCola said sternly. "Anyway...what you say to Kris after that?"

"That I didn't give a damn about why she didn't call me back."

"What she say?"

"Nothin cause I hung the phone up in her face...girl, I'm done with her ass. I shouldn't have had sex with her...but ain't nothin I can do about that now." Keleya continued to talk to JaCola until Jordan arrived, which was a few minutes before midnight. She got off the phone and opened the door for Jordan. They sat together and talked.

"I didn't think you were going to call me so I went to some girl's party," Jordan stated.

"Some girl?" Keleya asked.

"My cousin threw a party for one of her friends."

"Why would you think that? I told you I would call."

"Because it got late and...I don't know. But I missed you," Jordan said before pulling Keleya's legs on top of hers.

"You missed me?" Keleya asked skeptically. Jordan smiled and shook her head yes. When she leaned forward to kiss Keleya on the cheek, Keleya could smell the scent of Jordan's apartment and bath soap. "You took a shower?"

"I had to. I couldn't come see my woman smellin like a smokestack."

"Your woman? Is that who I am?"

"Is that who you wanna be?"

"What I want and what I'm ready for are two different things."

"Do you wanna be with me?"

Jordan's directness caught Keleya off guard. Although

they were spending a lot of time together, she hadn't seriously considered it. However, she wanted to be forthright about her feelings. "I feel like I am...but I have to take things slow," she replied after a moment.

"Because you just got out of a relationship?"

"That's part of it, but that's only a small part of it...this is just the way I feel."

"Keleya...I need to know that you wanna be here the same way that I wanna be here...and I gotta be honest with you, I'm falling for you...I know I just met you not too long ago, but that doesn't matter to me...if this is too much for you right now, be upfront with me. Let me know."

Keleya placed her feet back onto the floor and turned towards Jordan. "I'm not lookin for a woman I can be with for the next fifty years. I mean, if that's what it turns into I'm all for it...right now, I want a companion...someone to be with and confide in. And I want someone who's DDD free," she smiled. "No, but for real...Jordan, I wanna be with a woman I can grow to trust. That's important to me. So...if you feel the same way, then we're on the same page."

Jordan nodded her head in agreement. "We are." She rubbed along Keleya's leg and hand and said, "You look nice."

"Jordan...I got on a tank and tights."

"Why don't you ever let me compliment you? You need to work on that...you look good as hell."

Keleya stroked Jordan's locs. "What's good about me?"

Jordan licked her lips and said, "Everything...come here baby." Keleya stood and sat in Jordan's lap. Jordan ran her hands down the small of Keleya's back and up the curves of her thighs and hips as Keleya kissed her. She took hold of Keleya's legs and placed her back on the sectional. Then she parted Keleya's legs and placed herself between firm thighs.

Keleya could no longer fight the way she felt about Jordan

and her body was proving this. She enjoyed having a woman in her arms and she craved being desired. Everything about it—even the weight of Jordan's body—felt *so* good. Keleya was reaching the point of no return, but she kept going...freely. She ran her hands across Jordan's locs and back, holding tightly as Jordan kissed her neck. As soon as she released her embrace, Jordan proceeded to remove her shirt, almost exposing the medium sized tattoo on her waist. "Wait," Keleya said abruptly.

"What's wrong?" Jordan asked. Keleya pushed her shirt down and looked away. "Are you okay?" she asked as they sat upright.

Okay? Keleya felt fucking foolish! She couldn't get her rocks off because of the big ass tattoo of another woman's name. And she was afraid of what Jordan's reaction may have been. "I really, *really* want this...but I can't do this right now," she eventually said. "I'm sorry."

Jordan looked Keleya in her eyes. "You don't have anything to be sorry about." She waited a moment and continued. "She hurt you didn't she?" Keleya looked at Jordan for clarification. "Your ex."

"Yes...but that's not the issue right now," Keleya explained. She dropped her head in the palm of her hands and rubbed her forehand.

"What's wrong?"

"I'm fuckin worked up."

"Shit, how do you think I feel?" Jordan commented and they laughed.

"Oh my god." Keleya paused to exhale. "You got parts of my body at full salute...let's move on to somethin else so I can get this off my mind."

"Okay...why is it that every time I see you, you got a different do? When I met you, you were rockin twists, then you had a curly fro, and then it was slicked over to the side. Now your hair is long and straight."

Keleya laughed. "Leave me alone. I can't get my hair did?" she joked.

"I mean I like it. I've just never dated a woman with so many transitions," Jordan smiled. She ran her fingers across the hair that fell along Keleya's brow. "It looks nice." Keleya accepted the compliment by saying thanks. Then she lay across Jordan as they continued to talk. She flipped through the channels, using various programming to introduce random topics into the conversation. She stopped on a movie set in the city of New York. "You ever been to New York?" Jordan asked.

"The closest I've been to New York is Trenton. My Aunt Carolyn lived there for a while."

"That's your mother's sister?"

"Yeah." Keleya changed the channel to Lifetime, where a therapist asked the main character about fears.

Jordan rubbed Keleya's back and asked, "What do you fear? What makes you weak?"

Keleya turned to face Jordan. And after a moment of consideration, she answered, "Uncertainty…I don't like the unknown. And I don't like the lack of control that uncertainty brings in my life…what's your weakness?"

"Social networks."

"I'm serious."

Jordan laughed. "I am too." Then she exhaled and said, "Women."

"When you say women, what do you mean? Do you mean cheating?"

"No…I feel like I've been able to guide most aspects of my life. But when it comes to relationships, I've had nothin but love/hate experiences."

"Has it been one more than the other?"

"Yeah, the former…I'm like most Black women. I want commitment, respect…and trust…I want someone that's genuine…I want a woman that ain't always focused on the fact that we're lesbian identified. And I don't want someone who's into the scene cause I've been there and done that. I want a woman who recognizes the fact that we're both women… hell…I'm almost thirty."

"Thirty is young."

"I know. But that's not the way I feel about it…sometimes, I feel like I'm running out of time and I need to hurry up and fix this one thing…but anyway, I have a question for you. How do you see me? Am I like…another girlfriend? A rebound?"

"You're not a rebound Jordan…and don't take this the wrong way, but I can be by myself. I see you as…a new chapter in my life."

"When it ends do you think I'll still be in it?"

Keleya smiled and took Jordan's hand. "I'd like you to be."

Every time I see Jordan, my feelings for her grow. I really appreciate her sincerity and I feel like I learned more about her tonight than any other time we've spent together. We talked to 6:00 and then we got in my bed to go to sleep. I put my head on her arm and lay against her body while thinking about her…us. After what happened in my last relationship, I don't know what the future holds…but I'm willing to let this ride.

June 18th

"I AIN'T SEEN you in a month. And the few times we talked on the phone we was both too busy to say anything," JaCola stated. "What you been up to?"

"You know what I do," Keleya replied. "Work. Come home. See the fam. Work."

"Well…I'm bout to drop Maleek off. If you ain't doing nothin, I'll stop by there."

Although Keleya had reservations about JaCola's visit, she acquiesced to the proposition. After ending the call, she looked at Jordan whose head was resting on her shoulder. "That was JaCola?"

"Yeah. She's comin over," Keleya replied.

"I'll leave so you can spend some time with her."

"You don't have to leave."

"How would she feel if she walked in and just saw me sittin here?"

"You say that like we used to be together."

"Look, its cool," Jordan said, but Keleya sensed that she was disappointed. Jordan got up and kissed Keleya goodbye. "I'll call you tomorrow, okay?"

"Okay."

Keleya made a conscious effort to show no frustration

about the visit when JaCola arrived. The first thing Keleya noticed when she walked in was her hair. JaCola had it shaved even shorter to rock a bald fade, leaving just enough hair at the top to keep the curl pattern. It fit the shape of her face very well. "Look at you. I like your hair."

"Thank you," JaCola said as she sat opposite Keleya. "Ricky did it for me the other day…I told Maleek I was comin over here. He told me to tell you hello."

Keleya smiled. "Are you for real?"

"Yeah. You know that boy think he grown."

Keleya got up and walked to the kitchen. "I know you glad he's gettin older," she commented as she reflected on Maleek's birth. Keleya was in her first year of grad school, and JaCola would periodically call frantic about her upcoming due date. Rightfully so, she was scared and doubted her decision to become a single mother. "You want a pop?"

"What kind?" JaCola asked.

"Red Cream."

"Yeah." After Keleya handed her the soda and sat down, JaCola gazed at her friend. "So what you really been up to lately Ms. Smith?"

"I told you. How is Ricky?"

"Leya! Answer the question."

"If you wanna know something ask. I don't read minds."

"What's the business with you and Jordan? Y'all first went out in what…April? Then ya'll started hangin out. And ya'll went out with my sister and didn't invite me to—"

"You were at work JaCola!"

"Whatever! So what's going on? I know you doing more than going to work and comin home everyday cause when you were by yourself you was spendin your time with me and Maleek or Janya." JaCola paused, awaiting Keleya's response.

"We spend time together."

"What does that mean?"

"That means that we see each other whenever we can. Anything else you wanna know Ms. Harris?"

"Have you had sex with her?" JaCola asked without hesitation.

Keleya laughed. "Of all the things you could have asked me you gone ask me if I slept with her?"

"I wanna know," JaCola smiled.

"No…we're friendly, but not that friendly."

"Why not?"

"Damn! You asked me like there's somethin wrong with me waitin."

JaCola laughed and continued to question Keleya. "Has she been over here?"

"Yeah, of course."

"You must really like her to bring her over here."

"Why wouldn't I?"

"I'm just sayin. You don't feel weird bringin her in ya'lls old apartment?"

"Ya'll? People do it all the time Cola."

"I know people do," JaCola noted, "but I also know you." Keleya looked at the TV. She knew JaCola was right about her character. "Why haven't you had sex with her? Cause I will admit, she is attractive."

"Just because I like her and she's fine as hell don't mean I got to have sex with her."

"You have with other girls you liked…remember Shalonda? Veda? And—"

"I never had sex with Veda. And I ain't ready for all that right now."

"Cause of Kris?"

"Cause of *myself*…and what's up with you tryin to interrogate me?"

"I'm just askin. Hell, if I don't ask I won't know…so… why you like her?"

"Because she's…nice and I like nice women…she's a good listener. She's outgoing…she makes me laugh…she's smart and you know I *love* a smart female."

"I know."

"Right, the shit is sexy…and we have things in common."

"Well…I ain't gone lie. Jordan sounds a lot like Kris and she looks like her too."

Keleya shook her head in disagreement. "No, I think you…" She paused to check a text. *I'm at home. Ttyl. J.* "You say that because you don't know her. Believe me, they are two different people."

"So, where is this going?"

"It is what it is for right now."

"Well if you happy, I'm happy…when we gone get together and go out?"

"I don't know…we'll see," Keleya said half-heartedly.

JaCola may feel like I'm tryin to keep this one to myself…whatever that means…but I don't have a problem with extending Jordan into other aspects of my life, specifically my personal relationships. But emotionally, I have to take things one-step at a time.

June 21st

TODAY, INSTEAD OF going home after work, Jordan stopped by to see Keleya. She walked into the apartment and immediately sat down, no kiss. "What's wrong?" Keleya asked as she returned to the dining room table.

"I'm a little frustrated with some shit that just went down at work…but I'm cool. You must've left early today."

"Yeah. How you know?"

"I emailed you, but you didn't respond. So I figured you left early."

Keleya looked at her phone, realizing she hadn't checked her email in hours. "Yeah, I left and picked my niece up from daycare…Zana came and got her about thirty minutes ago."

"I would've liked to meet her," Jordan commented. Keleya continued to read through work documents and PowerPoint presentations, outlining tasks and deadlines in her planner. She heard Jordan stand up, but she didn't pay her much mind. "What's in this case?"

"What case?"

"The black one on the DVR?"

"DVDs…movies."

Jordan opened the case and flipped through the ninety-six titles. "Damn. I'm crushin on a pirate."

"Don't act new," Keleya smiled.

After a moment, Jordan laughed. "Yo, who has *Real Geniuses*, *Crooklyn*, *Saving Face*, *The Last Dragon*, *Finding Nemo*, *Teen Witch*, *Minority Report* and *Boyz n the Hood* in the same movie collection? I mean come on...*Karate Kid* and *School Daze*."

"Have you even seen *Saving Face*, *Teen Witch* or *Real Geniuses*?"

"Yeah," Jordan replied. "Guess that says somethin about me, huh?"

Keleya smiled and turned the page. A few minutes later, she closed her laptop, put the documents and planner away and sat beside Jordan on the floor. She caressed her locs and said, "You look tired Jordan."

"Damn. Only you can make the word tired sexy. Say my name again."

"You want me to go back over there?"

Jordan smiled, moved towards Keleya and kissed her sweetly. "You want me to stop?"

"Yes."

"Why?"

Despite the sexual attraction they shared, Keleya was on a noble mission to keep the lid on the cookie jar for as long as possible. "You know why," she responded.

Jordan leaned back against the chaise lounge. "I saw your friend yesterday."

The first person that came to Keleya's mind was Kris, but of course they'd never met. "JaCola?"

"Yeah."

"Where?"

"At Walmart."

"You haven't seen JaCola in months. You remembered her?"

"Not at first, but when she damn near hit me with a basket I did."

"How did that happen?"

"I was standing in line and noticed this girl tryin to beat this lady in line behind me. So of course, I kind of turned around to see who it was and then she called my name."

"What did she say?"

"She asked how I was doing and said that you were planning somethin for us to get together."

"No I'm not!"

"What? She lied about that?"

"She exaggerated about that. That is *not* what I told her."

"Well look, I'm glad it was JaCola and not Nkozan... Nsaza...your sister cause the last time I saw her she was flirtin with me," Jordan stated, referring to a day last week when Nkosazana randomly stopped by Keleya's apartment.

"It's N-ko-sa-zana," Keleya laughed. "And she was being Zana on ten."

"That shit don't bother you?"

"I don't know...I don't think I notice it anymore. She always been like that."

"Whose sister flirts with their sister's girlfriend?"

Keleya knew the question was rhetorical, but she answered anyway. "Nkosazana."

"And what's up with her name? I know it's an African name, but what does it mean and why?"

"Her father named her. It means princess...and my name is African too."

"Really? I learn somethin new about you everyday."

"You wouldn't know it by lookin at Zana, but her father is very African-centered. At some point when he was with my momma he gave her a book called *Sundiata*. You ever read it?

"*Sundiata*...no."

"Well, my momma read the book and liked the name Keleya. So she decided their next child, if a girl, would be named Keleya. Of course their relationship ended, but I guess my momma liked the name so much that she gave it to me anyway."

Although Jordan was tired, she stayed with me for the rest of the evening. We continued to talk about family and some of the dumb shit that we did growing up. I made dinner and we watched "Trading Places." She left around 11:30...and as usual, I can't wait to see her again.

June 22nd

AS ANTICIPATED, JACOLA sent Keleya a text the next day.

U busy? U still at work?
No and yes. What's up?
Saw ur girl at the store.
I heard.
What r ur plans for the wknd? Cardell can give us VIP.
U sure u wanna go there??? What's the other option?
I'm a single mother. I don't care. LOL.
Just let me know.
K. I'll call u when I leave.

After work, Keleya went to her mother's house to pick up dinner. She was glad that Rita called because she didn't want to cook or eat out that day. When Keleya walked in, Rita was pouring cabbage into two, medium containers. She wrapped cornbread in foil and placed the food in a plastic Kroger bag. "How your job going?" Rita asked as she tied the bag.

"It's alright, but it could be better," Keleya replied.

"Is it payin the bills?"

"Yes."

"Then it is better."

Keleya rolled her eyes. She was annoyed with her mother's attitude about employment. She seemed to believe that any job was a good job and that having a good salary equated to some kind of happiness. "Momma, just because I got a job don't mean that I like it."

"Well what would you rather be doing?" Rita asked. But Keleya couldn't answer the question because she didn't know. The only thing she was sure about was the fact that she found little satisfaction in the position. "What you doing when you leave here?"

"I'm going home. I'm tired."

"Your sister comin this weekend. You comin by?"

'Duh,' Keleya thought. "She comin Friday or Saturday?"

"Friday…you got plans?"

"I might go somewhere."

"You can still come by and see her and the babies…where you plan on going?"

"We're not sure yet."

"Who is we?"

"Me and some friends."

"You got a girlfriend now?"

"I didn't say a friend. I said some friends."

"Why you havin such as a hard time answerin questions today Leya?"

"Yes I do," Keleya answered.

"Why you keepin her such a secret? You gone tell me her name?"

"Jordan."

"Jordan? This is a woman right?"

Keleya gave a half laugh. "Umm…duh."

"Well, I didn't know now…a woman named Jordan."

"Momma it's not unusual."

"Who said?" Rita asked.

Keleya stood up and said, "Momma, I'm bout to go. I'll be back when Stacy gets here." Rita walked her daughter to the car while yelling across the street to greet a neighbor.

After pulling away, Keleya called Jordan. They hadn't talked, emailed or text because of the busy workday. As soon as Jordan answered the call, she said, "Let me call you back in a minute." She called back two minutes later and asked, "What you up to?"

"I'm on my way home."

"You just now leavin work?"

"No, I'm leavin my momma's house."

"Oh…I'm glad you called. I had to—hold on a second." Jordan clicked over for another minute. "Sorry about that."

"Are you busy?" Keleya asked annoyed.

"No…my momma is tryin to find somebody to pick my grandmother up after dialysis cause I won't be able to leave tomorrow."

"Jordan, just call me back."

"No, I'm good. I'll call her back later…you wanna come over here?" Jordan asked. Keleya was always in the mood to see Jordan, but today, she only wanted to go home and chill. "Why you so quiet?"

"J I wanna see you, but I'm tired as hell."

"Baby, I understand. Go home and get some rest."

Keleya and Jordan said their goodbyes and ended the call. When Keleya arrived at her apartment complex, she stopped by the mailbox. As she pulled up to the mailbox row, she heard another car park behind her, but she didn't pay the newcomer any attention. There were a few envelopes and several pieces of direct mail in the cubby. From time to time, she received mail for Kris. She agreed to text Kris about important mail. Otherwise, Kris would get it whenever. Keleya turned to head back to the car, realizing that the accompanying resident was Soria. She thought it was strange to run into her at this particular location given she never had before. As she walked pass, Keleya was nice enough to say hello. And just as she stepped off the sidewalk, Soria spoke back by calling her name. Keleya turned around to acknowledge her. "If you have any mail for Kris, you can give it to me," Soria stated.

"Excuse me?" Keleya asked with surprise.

Soria took two steps forward. "I said you can give me Kris' mail. She'll be by to see me anyway."

Keleya was taken aback by Soria's total disregard for her past with Kris and the disrespectful approach. "If that's the case, let her know to stop by and see me first," Keleya responded. Then she got in the car and left. While driving to her apartment, Keleya thought about the fact that she hadn't seen Soria in months. She'd seen Kris' car in the complex a few times, so she had an idea of what was going on between the two. But this run in with Soria confirmed her assumption.

I walked in the apartment and threw the mail on the coffee table. There was something in the stack for Kris, but I'll be damned if text her about it right now. I took a shower, got in the bed and flipped the channel to one of the satellite music stations. Maxwell's "Bad Habits" was playing. While lying across the bed, I thought about Soria...how she looks...the way she dresses...the way she acts...very Memphis. And then I recalled what I could remember about Jazmine...I realized Soria and Jazmine were pretty much the same girl. Then I thought about myself and how I am nothing like either one of them...and then I thought about Kris and how it is now obvious that she is attracted to women that are nothing like me...and that hurts.

June 24th

KELEYA WENT TO work an hour early to complete tasks that were overlooked or postponed due to the hectic workweek. She shared a large office with Leigh Ann, a twenty-eight-year-old University of Memphis graduate who worked in marketing as well. Approaching the office, Keleya could see an open door. She became a little disappointed by the fact that Leigh Ann was already at work. "Good morning," Keleya said as she stepped into the office.

"Good morning, you came to catch up too?"

"Yeah…unfortunately," Keleya said under her breath.

"I can't wait until all of this is over," Leigh Ann commented, referring to the fundraising activities the organization was implementing.

Keleya sat at her desk and turned towards Leigh Ann. "I know right."

"You know about the meeting today?"

"No, I haven't checked any emails that were sent past 4:00 yesterday. What time and about what?"

"At 11:00. I think we're gonna do a run down of the event and talk about the remainder of the week."

"Okay," is all Keleya said in response.

Ten minutes prior to the meeting, Jason, a development staff member, stepped into their office uninvited. "Hey you guys. You wanna walk with me to the meeting? I can't go alone."

"Sure," Leigh Ann replied, but Keleya didn't say a word.

"You gonna come with Keleya?" Jason asked loudly while sipping from his coffee mug.

"No, go ahead. I'll be there in a minute." When Keleya entered the meeting room there were seventeen people gathered around two adjoining conference tables. There were only two empty seats, so she sat next to Tanya, one of three African–American employees in an administrative or professional role.

"How you doing?" Tanya asked.

"Hey, I'm alright. Did you know about this?" Keleya inquired.

"Uh uhh," Tanya answered.

A few minutes later, the organization's president, Ed Tanner, commenced the meeting. He began with a brief report and encouraged the staff to keep up the good work. He commented about the fundraising activities and opened the floor for a question and answer period. There were a few questions and statements before Mary, a career counselor, mentioned the lack of representation from the Health Department. Tanner responded first. "It's been an objective of ours, every year, to invite as many relevant agencies and factions of the Memphis and Shelby County governments as we can. And starting this year, the marketing team has pushed those invites throughout the tri-state area. We reached out to Tipton County up north. Umm...Fayette County to the east. And then the...the neighboring counties in Mississippi and Arkansas. So we've definitely said join us. Did anyone contact the Health Department directly?"

Before Keleya could open her mouth to take ownership of the action, Jason spoke. "Yeah, I think that was Keleya's responsibility," he said and everyone looked at Keleya.

She undercut her eyes at Jason for a second and redirected her attention to Mary. "I talked to the director of the Health Department on two separate occasions. I talked to her on January 26th and again on February 26th if I recall correctly. I explained to her what were doing, why I felt it was important that the Department be present this week and then I gave her a personal invite. She expressed interest in the activities and said that if she could not attend herself, she would send representatives." 'Nough said,' Keleya thought as she pivoted the chair to face Tanner.

"Okay, any other questions or concerns?" Tanner asked.

Before departing ways at the conclusion of the meeting, Tanya turned to Keleya. "Girl, I know Jason didn't call himself tryin to call you out did he?"

"Who you tellin?" Keleya stated. "That was completely unnecessary. I don't need no emcee."

"Okaay," Tanya agreed.

After the meeting, the busy workday progressed as usual, but Keleya made sure to text Jordan. *Hey J. JaCola wants to know if we'll go to The City this weekend.* Jordan replied twenty minutes later. *Yeah. Angie asked me about that today. Call u later.* 'Damn,' Keleya thought. 'Them sisters know they can hound some folks.' She put her cell phone down and continued to analyze the organization's website traffic.

Around 3:45, Jason popped into the office again, but Leigh Ann wasn't there. "Hi Keleya," he said. "I just wanted to let you know that I meant no offense in the meeting today."

"So you know you were in the wrong?" Keleya noted.

"Sometimes I get a little ahead of myself."

"Right," Keleya responded before directing her attention to the ringing office phone. And because she no longer acknowledged Jason's presence, he quietly exited the office.

Keleya decided to go home for a moment before heading to the fundraising activity that evening. She exited the building, but before entering the parking lot someone called her name. She turned around and saw Jason walking towards her. "Do you have a second?" he asked.

"Yes."

"Well…I'll get straight to the point. There's an obvious tension between us and I'm not exactly sure where it stems from."

"And?"

"And I don't understand," Jason expressed. "I mean, what's the problem? I've been more than fair with you."

"Fair? What exactly is the other option Jason?"

"I'm just saying that it seems as if you have a…you just seem to be…I don't know, irritated by us."

"And how is that? Have you forgotten that you don't know anything about me other than my name, my job title, my race and my sex? So how can you make that call? If I am anything, I'm annoyed by *you*." Jason was silent, so Keleya continued. "Look, it's obvious that you and I have nothing in common. So if you can remember that I don't need anyone to speak for me and that I'm a competent adult, we can coexist."

After that, there was nothing more to be said. So I rolled my eyes to the best of my ability and walked away.

June 26th

KELEYA WAS ECSTATIC after wrapping up the last of the weeklong fundraising activities. She left the event and drove to her mother's house as planned. As she approached the house, she could see Nkosazana's car in the driveway. She hadn't talked to her sister in a few weeks, so they sat in the kitchen and talked while the rest of the family hung out in the den. "So what is Rod gone do?" Keleya asked. "Is he comin to get Janya?"

"That nigga ain't gone pick his daughter up. He feel like the only goddamn thing he got to do is pay child support... fuck him. He gone regret the shit one day," Nkosazana vented. "I don't wanna talk about him no more...what you plan on doing for the rest of the day?"

"I'm going to *The City*?"

"Why didn't you ask me if I wanted to go?" Nkosazana shouted. "Hell, I guess you get booed up again and can't hang out with your sister no more. When you going?"

"I don't know. I think 10:30. Cola is supposed to let me know."

"Text her and tell her I'm comin too. Is it VIP?" Keleya shook her head yes as she began the text. "You want me to ask Stacy if she wanna go?"

"Girl…please," Keleya said with little faith. "She not going." Nkosazana sprang out of the chair and pranced into the den to prove Keleya wrong. Keleya was eager to hear Stacy's response so she followed her sister, stopping in the doorway as Nkosazana sat beside Stacy.

"Momma, can you watch the children tonight? Cause me, Leya and Stacy going out."

"I'm doing what?" Stacy asked.

"You going out with us tonight," Nkosazana replied.

"No I'm not!" Stacy declared.

"If you need somethin to wear I can go home and get you an outfit," Nkosazana stated. "What time we going?"

"She said 11:00," Keleya replied.

"Zana, I'm not going," Stacy said with authority in her voice.

"You come down here every month and don't never go nowhere with us," Nkosazana claimed.

"Stacy, loosen up girl. You still young enough to go to the club," Rita commented, prompting Keleya and Nkosazana to look at each other and laugh.

"That ain't funny. I know I ain't old. Thirty-three is the new twenty-three," Stacy remarked.

"Look, it's only 6:30. I can go home and find you somethin to wear and then come back over here and you can get dressed. Then we'll pick Leya up."

Stacy took a moment to consider the plan. "Where we going?"

"To *The City*," Keleya responded. "It's downtown."

"And how long we gone be there?" Stacy asked next.

"Til the sun come up," Nkosazana replied.

"You shouldn't have said that," Rita laughed.

Stacy stood to walk to the kitchen. Before exiting, she announced, "I'll go, but I ain't wearin *nothin* from your closet.

I'll look to see what I brought, and if I don't have anything I'll run to the store."

"What you wearin Leya?" Nkosazana asked.

"I don't know."

"You don't know?" Nkosazana questioned.

"I don't have to prepare myself like you do. Girl, it ain't that serious."

"Umm, I forgot. You're off the market," Nkosazana commented. "Let Cola know it's two more, not just me."

Keleya stayed with her family for another hour. She went home to take a nap, but the vibrating cell phone disturbed her just as she fell into deep sleep. She rolled over and grabbed the phone off the nightstand. "You sleep?" Jordan asked after Keleya answered.

"I was."

"If you're tired, you should stay home. You had a lot going on this week...I can come over and see you."

Keleya rolled onto her back. "No...I'm going."

"You want me to pick you up?"

"No...I'm ridin with my sisters."

"Sisters?"

"Yeah. I'm surprised too."

"You sure you wanna go?"

"Yeah."

"Okay. I'll see you there."

When Keleya and her sisters entered *The City*, folks were packed in the club like sardines. But when they entered VIP, the space and air became less dense. And like the last time, JaCola had a table chock-full of alcohol and shot glasses. Cardell had given her a full set up. Angie, who saw them approach first, sat adjacent to her sister. And by the look in her eyes, she began drinking before she arrived. She had her arm around some woman that looked older than Stacy. Jordan sat across from Angie. Before sitting next to Jordan, Keleya embraced and kissed her hello. Nkosazana sat next to Keleya and Stacy sat opposite JaCola. After Nkosazana introduced Stacy and Angie introduced Quisha, JaCola and Angie initiated a long conversation with Stacy because they hadn't seen each other in several years. Nkosazana joined in and Quisha just listened. Keleya consumed herself with Jordan and Jordan did the same. "Did you wear this for me?" Jordan asked as she caressed Keleya's leg.

Keleya smiled. "No."

"Are you sure?" Jordan asked as she gawked at her cleavage.

"Sit back," Keleya said, pushing Jordan away.

"You and your sister look just alike."

Keleya looked at Stacy. "You think so?"

"Yeah...you dancin with me tonight?"

Keleya shook her head yes and noticed Cardell approaching the table. He spoke to the women before whispering in JaCola's ear. She subsequently stood and left with him. Keleya was so wrapped up into what was happening with JaCola that she didn't notice Jordan's hands slowly working their way up her thighs. "How many shots have you had?" she asked as she moved Jordan's hands to a more comfortable location.

"Two. You want one?"

"No," Keleya said, but Jordan ignored her response. She took a shot glass and placed it in front of Keleya. Lime wedges and salt were in the middle of the table. She poured Absolut into the glass and lifted the glass so that Keleya could take it.

When Angie saw Jordan holding the glass, she shouted, "Hold up! If you go, we all go."

"Shit, I'm down," Nkosazana said as she gave Stacy a shot glass too.

"Uh uhh," Stacy said before thrusting the glass to the middle of the table.

"Hell naw!" Angie shouted, sliding the glass back down the table. "You too Stacy!"

"I'll take one," Stacy gestured. "And don't ask me to do it again! What am I supposed to do?"

"Damn, stop actin fuckin square Stacy," Nkosazana said loudly. "You lick the back of your hand, pour the salt on it and then lick it." After watching her sister down the vodka and bite into the lime, Stacy quickly did the same and everyone else followed suit.

Before Keleya knew it, Jordan was refilling the glass. "No, I'm done...you tryin to get me drunk?"

"Match me. One more," Jordan insisted.

"Answer me first," Keleya demanded.

"Of course not. I just want you to enjoy yourself."

"I will," Keleya stated as she pushed the glass away.

JaCola returned a few minutes later to announce that a dance competition would soon begin on the main level and to ask if anyone wanted mixed drinks. Keleya requested a Bahama Mama and Nkosazana asked for a Sex on the Beach. When JaCola returned with the drinks, she moved her chair to the balcony railing to watch the show. Angie, Quisha and Stacy followed. Nkosazana, however, wanted to be closer to the stage so she went downstairs. Jordan and Keleya stayed seated at the table. After a shot and a mixed drink full of rum, Keleya was a little tipsy. Her sister came back almost half an hour later to join the group, so Keleya and Jordan decided they would too. They stood beside Nkosazana and looked into the large crowd. Several people were screaming because the dance off had turned into an all out vogue battle. There was a young Black male with no body fat on the stage wearing a pair of skinny jeans and a spaghetti strapped shirt that exposed his midriff. Every time he did the death drop, people fanned their arms and waved their hands while screaming at the top of their lungs "work bitch" or "fierce ass bitch"—actions reminiscent of church. They could see his competitors standing to the side of the stage, waiting to represent their crew or house. "You know who that is don't you?" Nkosazana asked her sister.

"On stage?" Keleya asked. "No."

"That's Sammy."

"Stop playin." Keleya gazed harder in order to recognize the former classmate, but she was standing too far away for a positive ID. Keleya thought it funny that Nkosazana would recognize him, given that she was years older. And even though she knew that her sister never forgot a face, she asked, "How you know that's him?"

"I seen him up close when I was down there."

The battle progressed and two additional competitors took the stage. One wore a pink tutu and white tights, whereas the second competitor was pretty butch queen. He fell five feet to the floor directly onto his back and the crowd went wild. "Ooh, death drops scare me," Keleya commented.

"I know right," Nkosazana agreed.

"I thought you went down there to participate," Jordan said to Nkosazana.

"Girl please. I can probably fall to the floor, but I guarantee I wouldn't be able to get my big ass up," Nkosazana joked.

Jordan was on the verge of commenting, but Angie called her name. After she stepped away, Keleya took notice of Stacy who was very much into the performances. "Look at your sister," she directed Nkosazana.

"Umm. I knew she would enjoy herself," Nkosazana stated. "I saw your boo downstairs." Keleya looked at her sister. "She had her arms wrapped around some broad."

"Did she see you?"

"Yeah. We talked for a second."

"You didn't tell her I was here did you?"

"No!" Nkosazana said, but Keleya did not believe her.

"What did you say?" Keleya asked with the expectation of full details.

"I said hello and how you been. That's it."

"And?" Keleya prodded.

"That's it!"

Kris and Soria. Keleya couldn't believe they were there. Tonight! The one night she decided to club. She slowly scanned the crowd below to see if she could spot the two, but she was disturbed when Jordan embraced her from behind. "You didn't hear me calling you?" Jordan asked.

"No," Keleya responded.

"What's wrong?"

"Nothing," Keleya said, quickly adjusting her demeanor. She tightened Jordan's embrace and they continued to watch the show.

By the time the battle ended, everyone had loosened up. And when they went back to the table, Keleya, along with JaCola, Nkosazana and Quisha, put back two more shots. Everyone else abstained. It didn't take long for Quisha and JaCola to become highly intoxicated, prompting a conversation about good sex when the DJ played *Best I Ever Had*. JaCola wanted all the women to participate in the conversation, so she demanded everyone's attention. "Listen…I'm gone start and ya'll gone follow in order. The best I ever had is when I got pregnant with Maleek. No joke," JaCola stated. And everyone fell out of her seat with laughter.

"Cola," Angie said laughing. "Don't *ever* tell nobody that shit again."

"Shut up!" JaCola yelled with barely opened eyes. "Go… it's yo turn."

When Angie stopped laughing, she proceeded with her best. "Man…I was twenty—"

"You gotta say best I ever had first," JaCola interrupted.

Angie stared at her sister for a moment. She turned her head and continued. "I was twenty when one of my momma's friends put it on me. She planted the seed for this tattoo," she said as she touched her neck.

"Yo, we all know you like your women seasoned," Jordan joked.

"What you tryin to say?" Quisha asked. Jordan smiled and took a sip of water.

"You can't go wrong with experience," Angie said before kissing Quisha on the cheek. "Go ahead baby."

"You damn right I'm seasoned. Well-marinated," Quisha smiled. "And the best I ever had was with Angie," she claimed. But everyone knew she was straight up lying.

Stacy, whose story surprised her sisters, explained that her best sexual experience was years ago in the back seat of a car with a former boyfriend. "It was Marvin…and don't tell my husband that," she said as she pointed at her sisters.

"You ain't got to worry about me sayin shit," Nkosazana stated. "You know I don't like him."

Stacy rolled and her eyes and said, "Just go."

"Hell…I done had that good yank. So I can't name just one," Nkosazana remarked. And everyone who knew her well could vouch for the validity of that statement. "But I can give ya'll some tips instead though."

"Umm, no ma'am," Stacy said shaking her head. "Let's just move on."

"JaCola. Best ever, hands down…last night," Jordan smiled.

"What?" JaCola laughed.

"I heard that!" Nkosazana yelled. "Lil sis doing the damn thing." Everyone laughed and looked at Keleya.

"First of all," Keleya said laughing, "not a damn thing

ACCEPT THE UNEXPECTED

happened last night. So you need to come correct real quick," she said to Jordan.

Jordan smiled and continued. "Sophomore year in the rain. That's all I'm sayin."

"Damn," Angie exclaimed. "Sounds like somebody need to get on the grind," she said while smiling at Keleya.

Keleya looked at Angie and mouthed 'whatever' as Jordan placed her arm around Keleya. "You can set the record tonight," Jordan whispered in her ear. Keleya leaned back and looked in her eyes.

"Break that shit up," JaCola said snapping her fingers. "Go ahead Leya." Keleya kissed Jordan on the lips and laughed. Then she pissed everyone off by declining her turn. After that, Keleya, JaCola and Quisha drank more, but they did so for different reasons. JaCola and Quisha drank for early arousal, preparing for the night's sexual festivities, whereas Keleya drank to drown thoughts of Kris and Soria and to wash away the stress of a long workweek. She was even prepared to drink away her celibacy. She knew it was emotionally irresponsible, but she continued with free will.

The seven women talked more, laughed more, and with the exception of Quisha—who gave a private lap dance—they danced more. They all left *The City* and parted ways at 3:00. And everyone was highly surprised when JaCola got in the car with Angie and Quisha, not Cardell.

Jordan walked me to the car, held me in her arms and kissed me goodnight. Although I seemed collected, I allowed my drunken stupor to decide that the night was not over for me. So instead of getting in the car and leaving with my sisters, I walked away and went home with Jordan.

June 28th

TODAY'S AWAKENING BROUGHT forth a new day. And for that Keleya was grateful. But the day also meant the promise of another workweek. Although she'd only worked for her current employer for eleven months, the monotony of a nine to five began to weigh heavily on her spirit.

Keleya got out of her car and headed to the office. It was becoming an over traveled route, so much so that she'd semi–consciously counted the steps between each segment. After a total of 207 steps, she sat at the desk and would hold her breath for the remainder of the day. A few minutes before her lunch break she received a call on the office phone. "Hey Cola," she answered.

"You busy?"

"No. I'm just sittin here."

"I should've called you yesterday, but I was too damn sick to do anything."

"You had a hangover?"

"Hell yeah! And I still don't feel right."

"Did you take anything?"

"Yeah, but my stomach still messed up...anyway, what time did you get home yesterday?" JaCola asked in a chipper voice.

'I knew it was coming,' Keleya thought. "About 1:00."

"And what did you do until 1:00? That's a long time to be over somebody's house," JaCola said in the same manner.

"Girl, I can't talk about that right now."

"Why not?" JaCola asked, reverting back to her normal tone of voice. "Is that White girl in there?"

"No. And there are just some things that need to be discussed at home. Plus, folks round here nosey."

"Well, I'll call you after I go home and lay down for a while girl."

"Alright." Keleya hung up the phone and stared at the computer screen. It was lunchtime, but she was not in the mood to move or see coworkers. So she shut the office door and listened to the radio while surfing the Internet. Twenty minutes into the faux retreat, she received an unusually early call from Jordan. She answered her cell phone anxious to know purpose of the call.

"Keleya you busy?" Jordan asked.

"No."

"Did I leave my computer charger at your apartment yesterday?"

"Hmm...no."

"Damn...that means one of these bad ass girls around here took my shit."

Keleya was quiet for a moment. This was the first time she'd heard Jordan express frustration. "Jordan."

"What?"

"You shouldn't talk about those girls like that."

"Yeah...you right, I'm sorry. My computer is almost dead...hold on a second." She briefly placed Keleya on hold and then clicked over again. "Hello?"

"I'm here."

"I'm pissed off cause I need my computer for a meeting,

but I'll figure somethin out."

"Do you want me to go to Apple and get you another one when I leave? I mean I know you need it now, but I can get it if you want me to."

"Yeah. If you don't mind I appreciate it. I'll come get it this evening."

"Alright."

"Kelee–baby, how you doing?"

Keleya smiled upon hearing her new pet name, but her expression changed when she answered the question. "Honestly…not good."

"What's wrong?"

Keleya exhaled. "We can talk about it later."

"Are you okay?"

"Yeah…I just don't wanna get into it right now."

"Okay. I don't know what time I'm leaving here, but I'll see you later."

I ended the call and turned my attention back to the computer screen. Displayed was an alphabetized listing of one-bedroom apartments in Miami and surrounding areas. I stared at the page, reflecting on my pre and post–graduation ambitions—one of which included moving to Miami. Kris, on the other hand, wanted to move back home. So now I'm fucking stuck in Memphis! And thinking about this made my body tense, so I closed the browser and rest my head on the desk hoping no one would knock on the office door before the end of the day.

• • •

Keleya walked through her apartment door at 6:30. She placed the bag with the charger on the kitchen table along with her purse. She walked into her bedroom to wash her face and change clothes. She was not in the mood for anything, so she wrapped herself in a blanket and watched TV. Keleya knew JaCola would call at any minute, but she allowed herself to relax by listening to the sound of the hypnotizing rain, subsequently falling asleep. Almost an hour later her phone rang, but she didn't open her eyes. She just felt across the couch cushion for the phone and answered the call. "Hi...is this Keleya?" a woman asked.

"Yes...who is this?"

"This is Veda."

Keleya's eyes popped open. "Hey." She wanted to say more, but was at a loss for words.

"Is this a good time? If not, I can call back."

"No, you're good." Keleya removed the blanket and placed her feet on the floor.

"I know I'm the last person in the world you expected a call from," Veda commented.

"How'd you get my number?"

"From a friend of a friend who knows Kriston."

Keleya didn't know how to respond so she asked, "How have you been?"

"Good, things have been very good for me," Veda replied. "I called because I'll be in Memphis next week. I know that it's sort of last minute to call and spring this on you, but I wanted to know if you'd like to get together while I'm in town...of course, if you're available."

"Yeah, that's cool...just let me know when and where."

"Okay. After I get a few things scheduled, I'll call you back or text you."

After saying their goodbyes, Keleya got up and went to the bathroom. When she returned to the great room, her phone rang again. "Hey Cola."

"You at home?" JaCola asked.

"Yeah."

"Sounds like you at the store or somethin."

"No, that's the TV." Keleya grabbed the remote control to decrease the volume.

"Jordan over there?"

"No."

"Umm...that's a shock."

"I wouldn't have answered the phone if she was over here."

"What? I bet you do be doing me like that."

'Sometimes,' Keleya thought. "No, I don't...anyway, guess who just called me?"

"Kris?" JaCola guessed.

"No!"

"If it wasn't her, I don't know."

"Veda," Keleya revealed.

"Veda!"

"Yep."

"And what the hell did Ms. I'm-Too-Good-For-You say?"

"She said she'll be in Memphis sometime next week and wanted to know if I'd meet her."

"What? Uh uhh! I hope you said no."

"You know I didn't."

"Well when you see her, cuss the bitch out...so what did you do til 1:00?"

"We didn't have sex JaCola," Keleya replied. She knew JaCola would eventually ask if not previously told. "Hello?"

"I'm here," JaCola replied. "I'm waitin on you to tell me why not."

"Cause I was too fuckin intoxicated! And Jordan wouldn't take advantage of me."

"You wanted her to take advantage of you?"

"No, that came out wrong. What I mean is that I was too drunk to have sex cause all I wanted to do was go to sleep.

Even though I was wasted, Jordan didn't wanna have sex with me…actually, I can't say if she wanted to, she just didn't."

"How do you know she didn't?"

"Cause I know! I don't have memory lapses like you when I drink."

"So what happened?"

"Nothin. I went to her apartment, she gave me a shirt to sleep in and I went to sleep. I can't tell you when she went to sleep or when she got up. I just know I woke up around noon…I stayed over there for about an hour and she brought me home."

"You so lame!"

Keleya laughed. "Whatever! Don't get mad at me cause I can keep it closed longer than you." JaCola laughed. "You feel any better?"

"Mmm hmm. When I picked Maleek up from daycare, I took him over his granny house and came home to lay down."

"Hold on Cola." Keleya flashed the call to talk to Jordan and returned to the conservation with her friend. "Cola."

"Please don't tell me that was Veda."

"No, that's my boo. She outside. Bye."

"Oh my god! Bye!"

Keleya got up and opened the door. "You just got up?" Jordan asked as she sat and moved the blanket.

"No, I was on the phone when you called."

"You feel any better?"

"Yeah…sort of…this girl I used to talk to called out the blue and asked if I would be available to get together next week. And then I talked to JaCola, so that kind of took my mind off things…how was the meeting? Did it work out?"

"Yeah. I had just enough time to get the files off before it went dead. I had to change the meeting location because of that too…but it's all good…so…what's up with earlier today?

You had a bad day at work?"

"No. Work was the same ol same. I just...I hate my job. Actually...I don't hate my job. I like the work I do, I just don't want to do the work at work because then I'm working...does that make sense?"

"Not really."

"Okay, I don't hate my job. I have a good position and it's good experience. I just don't like the idea of working. And I especially don't like working for somebody else. But I know I have to work...and when I go to work, I do a good job. And that's it. I go to work and pay my bills and that's it. And that shit is startin to get real old, real fast. You understand what I'm sayin now?"

"Yeah...a lot of people feel that way."

"Hell, I know Jordan. But does it affect them like me?"

"Yes and no," Jordan replied. "The tone of your voice when I asked how you were doing was more than what you just told me. What I heard on the phone was damn near scary... I'm not tryin to mitigate the way you feel, I'm just asking why." Keleya wanted to talk to Jordan about the way she felt, but somehow or another that meant talking about Kris. So she omitted as much as she could without seeming distant as she explained these feelings. And she told Jordan that despite everything she had, she was still discontent. "I don't think leavin Memphis is a solution," Jordan responded. "I mean it could be—and I know that's what you want to do—but to me it sounds like you're kind of lost." Lost? Lost! All of the sudden, something inside Keleya sparked. Before Jordan said it, she couldn't put a name to it. But Jordan was right. *Lost* was right. "Find yourself," Jordan continued. "Find somethin that gives you some kind of purpose...what's somethin you've always wanted to do?"

"When I was in school, I volunteered for a while at a

GLBTQ youth center. It was like a safe haven. Doing somethin like that again has always kind of been in the back of mind."

"What are you waitin on?"

"I don't know…I pushed my plans to the backseat to be accommodating in my last relationship…I got side tracked and I haven't found my way back I guess. And…" Keleya paused and stared at the floor.

"You okay?"

Keleya shook her head yes. "I have some things to think about, but I'm good."

After Jordan gave me a long and comforting hug, I got up and went to my room to change clothes. We left and drove to Carson's. Once there, she asked me about the girl I used to talk to. I knew she would ask, so I explained that I met Veda fall semester freshmen year and that we were together for a little over a year before I got with Kris. And I explained that I hadn't actually seen or talked to Veda in five years. Jordan asked why she would randomly call years later. Of course, I don't know. But I guess I'll find out.

July 9th

VEDA WAS A woman of her word. She called Keleya two days later to designate a day, time and place for their rendezvous. And the scheduled date worked well for Jordan because she could spend the time with the other women in her life she'd been neglecting for weeks.

Veda asked Keleya to meet her in the lobby of *The Regatta*. Why Veda would come to Memphis and want to eat there— of all the places to eat in the city—Keleya didn't understand. After she entered the hotel, it didn't take long to spot Veda. Veda smiled and greeted Keleya with a hug before escorting her to one of the hotel's eateries. As they walked to the grill, Keleya thought about how much Veda had matured. But she was still charming and outgoing like Keleya remembered, and she was still one fine ass Black woman.

Once at the grill, they didn't wait for seating because Veda had already made reservations. After placing their orders and a few minutes of small talk, Keleya asked why Veda chose the location. "I'm staying here," Veda explained. "I didn't know of any other places in the city. I know I could have asked you, but I didn't think it was that big of a deal. Why? You don't like it?"

"It's not my thing, but it's fine. So, what brings you to the M. Veda?"

"Work. I'm an apparel buyer for a retailer in Atlanta."

"So you're still in Atlanta?"

"Yeah. Haven't left yet."

"You ever plan on going back to D.C.?" Keleya asked.

"One day, but not anytime soon. I wanna stay in this position for a few more years." Keleya and Veda continued to talk about their jobs. Keleya explained what she did and asked where Veda finished undergrad. Veda asked about UTK and then they talked a little about relationships...family...and some of their ambitions such as traveling. Veda was such a different woman. Keleya tried to catch a familiar mannerism or expression, but for the most part, Veda had transformed into the woman she always wanted to be. After finishing their meals, Veda insisted on paying the bill and the tip. And because Keleya didn't like anything she ate, she let her pay. "What are your plans for the rest of the evening?" Veda asked.

"No plans. I'm going home."

"You should come up for a while. We can order drinks."

Keleya considered the invitation for a moment. And then she said okay because she'd never been in or through the renowned hotel. They left the restaurant and rode the elevator to the tenth floor. Veda opened the door with the keycard and allowed Keleya to enter first. Keleya took a few steps into the well-appointed room and looked around. Veda was staying in an executive suite. "What kind of job did you say you have again?" Keleya asked.

"I have a good job," Veda responded as she took off five-inch pumps.

"No, you have a damn good job," Keleya stated as she sat on the sofa.

Veda joined Keleya and grabbed the drink menu from the table. She ordered an apple daiquiri for Keleya and a martini for herself. After the drinks arrived and after a few minutes of conversation, Veda began to seek answers for the questions she'd wondered about over the past five years. "So...I wanna know about Kriston. I remember the two of you got together about a month before I left."

"Yeah, I met her through a mutual friend when we were together," Keleya explained. Veda smiled. "That was like March of that year. From that point on, I would see her around campus, and there were two or three occasions that we were at Gary's apartment at the same time. You remember him?"

"Yeah."

"And then around July we started to kick it exclusively, and then we got together New Year's Eve."

"Who initiated?"

"I did."

"What happened?"

"We had way too much to drink and I kissed her. She said she wanted to be with me and I said okay. Neither one of us was serious about it, but a few days after that we talked and made it official."

"And you stayed together until this year?"

"Yeah, until February...what about Marchelle? It's Marchelle right?"

Veda shook her head yes. "We're off and on. Right now, we're off." Veda stood and walked to the phone to order another round of drinks. "You want another one?"

"No, I'm good."

"You sure? You don't want anything?"

"Well...order me a Sprite please."

"I like Marchelle, but she doesn't know the definition of fidelity," Veda said as she sat and crossed her legs. "I wanna be with her and her only. So when Marchelle wants to be exclusive, she's with me. And when she doesn't, she leaves." The drinks came and Veda continued to sip. And after fifteen minutes, she went from sober to tipsy and flirtatious. "What about your girlfriend? How did you meet Jordan?"

"Through a mutual friend."

"Do you meet all your women through mutual friends?"

Keleya laughed. "I didn't meet you through a mutual friend...JaCola's sister thought we'd be compatible. We met and things went from there."

"How long have you been together?"

"Unofficially, a little over two months. Officially, almost a month."

"Awe, you're newbies."

Keleya laughed, but at this point she was tired of beating around the bush. "Veda, why did you call me? Why am I here?"

"I wanted to see an old friend," Veda smiled. When she realized Keleya wasn't amused, she changed to a more solemn expression. "I left on bad terms. And I've thought about you from time to time over the years."

"Did you find what you were looking for?"

"What do you mean?" Veda asked.

"You left and went to Atlanta in pursuit of the glam life. You wanted to be a socialite...so you broke up with me because I was too ordinary. Remember? I didn't want to be on the A-list like you."

Veda was silent and looked slightly embarrassed. "Yes...I did find what I was looking for. But it didn't come without regrets...I was wrong for what I said to you...I ended the relationship, but I didn't have to disrespect you. And for that I apologize."

"So you called me to what? Mend fences? Clear your conscience?"

Veda sat her glass on the table and looked Keleya directly in her eyes. "I called because we have unfinished business."

Keleya looked at Veda. She felt like Veda was finally being

honest, and she knew *exactly* what Veda was implying. "Do you really think that after five years you can call, invite me to this room and then seduce me?"

Veda moved across the sofa to sit closer to Keleya. "I know we were only together for a year. We were young and our relationship was just one of several…but I'm not the same person and I know that you can see that…one day I was forced to examine my life and to list those I've hurt. And do you know who was at the top of the list for people I've hurt? *You*. And when I thought about what I did, I realized it was fucked up. After that, I was asked to think about people who have taken an interest in the hurt that I've experienced from others. And do you know who was at the top of that list? *You*. You were the only person, *ever*, who talked to me about my mother's murder and all the pain that I carried inside. You were the only person who ever expressed genuine interest in the way that I felt about her and what happened. And despite me hurting you—which I later learned was projection—I realized that even though I hadn't seen you in years, you held a special place in my heart."

Keleya took a few seconds to reflect on what Veda said. "If that's what I did for you, I'm glad for it. But what are you trying to do now? Return the favor?"

"Yes…if you let me."

Keleya rubbed across her hairline and closed her eyes for a second to digest Veda's offer. And when she opened them, Veda kissed her. After Keleya got past the shock and noticed how soft Veda's lips were, she kissed her back. She knew she was stupid for doing it, but she did it anyway. But it ended when she realized that Veda was unbuttoning her own blouse. "Stop…I'm not doing this," Keleya said as she pulled back.

"Because of Jordan?" Veda asked as she touched Keleya's thighs. "If you had any real feelings for her, you wouldn't be here right now."

Keleya looked at Veda who was absolutely beautiful. She was kissing a beautifully browned sister with luscious, partially exposed breasts. And Veda was down for *anything*. So Keleya moved towards Veda to touch her lovely face and to adore and kiss her full lips. Several seconds into the indulgence Keleya stopped. "Veda, I'm not in the business of turning people's regrets into satisfaction."

After saying that, I stood and left.

July 24th

DONYELLE MADE THE approximate two-hour trip to visit her cousin for the weekend. When she pulled into the parking space in front of Keleya's apartment, she called inside to announce her arrival. "Leya you sleep?" Donyelle asked.

"No, I'm up."

"I'm sittin in front of your door."

"Oh, okay." Keleya hung up the phone and walked outside to meet her cousin. "What's up cuzzo? Why you leave so early?"

"I didn't plan on it," Donyelle replied as they walked into the apartment. "I woke up at 7:00 and said I might as well get ready and leave."

"You stayin to Monday?"

"Yeah. I got class on Tuesday, so I'll leave when you go to work."

Keleya shook her head okay. "You want somethin to eat? I went to the store and bought some stuff to make breakfast yesterday."

"Yeah, but you gone make it right?"

"Of course. I don't need you wastin my money," Keleya smiled. A few minutes later, she went to the kitchen to make scrambled eggs, pancakes and turkey bacon.

"So what's the plan for the weekend?" Donyelle asked.

"I don't know…I really don't wanna go nowhere today. But we can go out tomorrow if you want to…sooo…I can cook and invite JaCola, my sister and Jordan over."

"Sounds good to me."

After breakfast, Donyelle stretched out on the sectional to take a nap. Keleya went into her bedroom to call JaCola and Nkosazana. Then she called Jordan. "You sleep?"

"Yeah," Jordan said groggily.

"Call me when you get up."

"I'm up now…what's up?"

"DD is here. I plan on cookin tonight and wanted to invite you over."

"What time?"

"7:00, 7:30."

"Alright. I'll call you back in a few hours."

Keleya got under her microsuede comforter and fell asleep. An hour and a half later, she woke up and got dressed. After DD was ready, the cousins went to the mall for a mani and pedi. On their way back to the apartment, they stopped by the grocery store to purchase a few items for the evening's gathering.

JaCola arrived first. She hadn't seen Donyelle since Keleya's high school graduation. And given that both Donyelle and JaCola were loquacious women, they conversed back and forth as Keleya went into the kitchen to prepare the meal. When JaCola opened the door for Jordan a few minutes before 8:00, Keleya exited the kitchen to introduce Jordan and Donyelle to each other. Afterwards, she returned to the kitchen and Jordan followed. "I brought you somethin," Jordan said after kissing Keleya on the cheek.

"What?"

"I'll give it to you later."

Keleya smiled and said, "Okay…go sit down. I don't

like folks in the kitchen when I cook." Jordan left and Keleya remained in the kitchen preparing rotel, Swedish meatballs, fried wings and Buffalo wings garnished with carrots and celery. Although JaCola didn't want to help, she asked Keleya if she needed any assistance. "No I'm good," Keleya yelled. When the food was almost done, Keleya blended apple margaritas and placed the mixture in the freezer. She was now at a point where she could take a break, so she left the stove and joined the other women.

"Leya where your sister at?" Donyelle asked.

"I talked to her this morning. Whether or not she's comin I don't know."

"Is she not comin because of her daughter?"

"Girl, I don't know…I guess I should check my phone to see if she called." Keleya got up and walked to her bedroom to see if Nkosazana had contacted her. She had no missed calls, but there was a text from Veda. *I've been thinking about you. Your kiss is unforgettable. Call me when you can.* Keleya stared into the distance for a moment. She didn't understand why Veda held such strong romantic feelings for her given that their past relationship was virtually platonic. She thought about replying with a message that would sever all ties, but Jordan walked into the bedroom. She sat on the bed and asked if Nkosazana had called. Keleya shook her head no.

"Are you going to call her?" Jordan asked.

"No." Keleya unplugged her phone from the charger and sat next to Jordan.

"You know, I thought that your cousin was part of your mother's family."

Keleya shook her head no. "She's my father's niece."

"I didn't know you had a relationship with any of his relatives."

"I don't…just DD," Keleya explained. "What did you

bring me?" Jordan reached into her back pocket, pulled out two sheets of paper that were folded into quarters and handed them to Keleya. Keleya opened the stapled papers, but before she could read it, JaCola stepped into the doorway.

"Leya, you want me to check the food?"

"Yeah. Can you turn the rotel off and take the other stuff out the oven?" After JaCola left, Keleya read what was in her hands. It was an abbreviated request for proposal from an agency that funds mentorship programs. "What is this about?"

"An organization that helps establish mentorship programs for GLBTQ youth of color. You can go to the website to get more details on submitting a grant proposal."

Keleya looked at the information again. "The deadline is August 31st Jordan!"

"I know…so look at it and think about it."

"Okay…thanks." Keleya placed the papers on the dresser and left the room with Jordan.

After the women ate and enjoyed mixed drinks, Donyelle and JaCola got comfortable on the sectional. Jordan sat on the floor in between Keleya's legs as they all talked back and forth. JaCola was growing tired of Keleya and Jordan's kissy face and affection so she got up and went to the kitchen. She took another bottle of Smirnoff out the refrigerator and talked to Donyelle. "You talkin to anybody right now?"

"Yeah. I've been in a relationship for about a year now," Donyelle responded.

"What's his name?"

"His name? Umm…I only do women."

"My fault! Guess I'm the only one in here who likes men," JaCola stated loudly.

"You've never liked a woman?" Jordan asked.

"No," JaCola replied.

"Never?" Jordan questioned.

"No…hell, ask Leya. She can tell you that."

"Just because I've never seen you with a woman doesn't mean you've never had feelings for one," Keleya remarked. JaCola was a little upset by her response, but she concealed this emotion and looked away.

"So you've never had sex with a woman?" Jordan asked and smiled.

"No!" JaCola responded, almost chocking. "I can't believe you just asked me that."

"You ever kissed a woman?"

"No!" JaCola answered again.

"You've never wanted to kiss or have sex with a woman?"

JaCola laughed. "What part of the N or the O don't you understand?"

"I asked if you've ever wanted to."

"No! I never have."

"I find that hard to believe. Most women I've met either like women or have fooled around with one at least once. Or they've considered it."

"Yeah, me too," Donyelle agreed.

"Or even if they don't admit it," Jordan continued, "they've found at least one woman attractive before."

"Good for you," JaCola replied. "But no, I've *never* wanted to be with a woman."

"So you date men exclusively?" Jordan asked.

"Yes!" JaCola laughed. "Only men."

"Only men? So you'll date a White boy?" Donyelle asked.

"No, I don't date outside my race. And why the hell am I being grilled? Have you ever had sex with a man? Do you date White girls?" JaCola asked Donyelle.

Donyelle looked disgusted. "Hell no and no!" she responded and everyone laughed. "What about you Jordan?

I already know Leya's a gold star, so have you ever had sex with a dude?"

"Umm, DD," Keleya said before Jordan answered. "Why would you say that? You know I don't like that term."

"I asked *her* the question," Donyelle responded, pointing to Jordan.

"What's a gold star?" Jordan asked.

"Basically dick free zone," JaCola replied. "That's what we call ya'll leslies that ain't fucked a man before."

"You put it more raw than I would, but that's what it means," Donyelle said.

"And what's a leslie?" Jordan asked.

"You!" Donyelle answered. "Look now, I'm askin the questions! Jordan, have you did the do with a dude?"

"Yes, I have."

"Uhh! I hope that was a *long* time ago," Donyelle said and they laughed. "Next question. Have you ever been with a White girl?"

"Yes."

"You have?" Donyelle asked again.

"Yeah. When I was twenty-two, I—"

"Wait, wait, wait!" Keleya interrupted. "*Please* don't give details."

"You didn't know about that?" JaCola asked.

"No," Keleya replied. "And I don't wanna know. So you need to change the subject before I start to feel differently about you."

Jordan laughed. "Okay...I'll throw somethin on the table. I wanna hear from your cousin and your best friend about you in past relationships."

"No ma'am," Keleya shouted. "No, let's talk about somethin else."

JaCola laughed. "I don't know about DD, but I'm talkin bout this! What you wanna know? Cause I'll tell it. You wanna know about Shalonda, Tay, Veda or Kris. Ooh! And hold up now. I forgot about Toeraysha. I remember her ass cause her momma spelled out every syllable in her name."

"Cola you don't need to talk," Keleya stated. "You spelled Maleek with two E's." Everyone, except JaCola laughed.

"Anyway!" JaCola said as she rolled her eyes. "What you wanna know? Cause if you think her ass is a saint, shiiit!"

Keleya stood up, walked to JaCola and snatched the Smirnoff from her hand. "I forgot yo ass can't hold liquor," Keleya commented. While JaCola, Donyelle and Jordan were dying with laughter, Keleya went into the kitchen and sat the bottle in the sink. And after she returned, she said, "Jordan, if there's anything you wanna know you can ask me."

"I know," Jordan stated. "But I don't want the shit filtered."

JaCola laughed. "Let's start with the first one. You know about Shalonda?"

"Yeah," Jordan replied. "We saw her once."

"Really? So you know that's who she lost her virginity to?"

"No," Jordan said as she looked at Keleya. "I didn't know that."

"They fucked around in 10th, 11th and 12th grade. I liked her. They were cute together. But that ended when Leya started fuckin around with this hard-core ass stud named Tay in 12th grade. Then she left and went to Knoxville. And when she got there she started fuckin around with a girl from Memphis. That was Toeraysha. From my understanding, that relationship was about nothing but sex. Toeraysha was cute, but she was a hot ass mess. And she almost got Leya arrested once. And next was Veda. You know about Veda?"

"Yeah," Jordan replied.

"We talk Cola," Keleya added.

"Hell, I'm just askin. Anyway! Veda was a bitch. I don't give a good goddamn how fine she was Leya, she was a bitch. And I don't know what attracted you to her or why ya'll were together for a year or however long it was." Keleya shook her head. "Moving on...and then there was Kris," JaCola smiled and Donyelle laughed.

"What's so funny?" Jordan asked.

"I don't mean to be rude, but I can't believe they ain't together no more," Donyelle replied. The response pissed Keleya off, but she kept her cool.

"Why not?" Jordan asked.

"Cause they were fuckin love birds. But you know what's even funnier?"

"What?" Jordan asked.

Before Donyelle answered, Keleya silently mouthed 'no,' hoping Donyelle would not go there. But Donyelle laughed and ignored her cousin. "Ya'll are *a lot* alike."

"I said the same thing!" JaCola commented as she simultaneously slapped her leg.

"Mmm hmm," Donyelle continued. "Ya'll about the same height, same body type, same—"

"Oh my god!" Keleya interrupted. She rubbed her forehead and said, "I knew I shouldn't have brought ya'll together...it's time for both of ya'll to go home."

Jordan laughed. "Is this really makin you that uncomfortable?"

"Yes!" Keleya shouted. After they heard her plea and changed the subject, they were all able to enjoy themselves.

When JaCola left at 1:00, Keleya and Jordan went into the bedroom while Donyelle chilled and talked on the phone. Jordan rest her body on Keleya's as they talked. "I like your cousin. She's cool," Jordan commented.

"I'm glad you came over...sort of," Keleya laughed.

"Why sort of?"

"Cause…you didn't have to ask them that."

"Kelee-baby, you don't like to talk about your past do you?"

"I don't mind talkin about my past. I just don't wanna hear about it through other people."

"Look, we were just havin fun. What you need to be thinkin about is that proposal so you can get that money…I think it's somethin you could and should do."

Keleya ran her fingers through Jordan's locs. "I don't need to think about it."

"And why is that?"

"Because I'm going to do it."

When Jordan left an hour later, I talked to DD for a minute and then got in the bed to think about this possible mentorship program. It's something that I actually wouldn't mind pursing. And I loved the fact that Jordan was thinking about my well-being…she believes in me…now I need to do the same.

August 7th

KELEYA HADN'T SEEN Jordan in a few days, so she left home late morning to spend the day with her. She got to Jordan's apartment fifteen minutes later and knocked on the door. "Why you knockin on the door? Why didn't you call me?" Jordan asked.

"I wanted to," Keleya replied as she hugged Jordan and walked into the apartment. After sitting her purse on the end table, she sat and removed her sandals.

"I thought you were going to call me back last night."

"I planned on it, but I stayed up all night researching recruitment methods."

Jordan sat beside Keleya and gave her a kiss. "How is the writing going?"

"It's going...hell, I feel like I'm writing a strategic plan. I just need to pull some things together and call a few more people...and I really need to talk to someone who can help me kind of flesh out operations before I send it in next week."

"You should talk to Renée?"

"The woman you work with?"

"Yeah. That's the area she works in. I can let her know that you'll contact her."

"Okay...thanks."

Jordan stood and asked Keleya to come into the bedroom while she took a shower. Keleya laid across Jordan's bed and text Donyelle to pass time. But when Jordan came out wearing only a pair of basketball shorts and a black sports bra, Keleya quickly redirected her attention.

As Jordan ironed clothes, Keleya tried her best to look directly in her face. She took a few deep breaths to suppress any forthcoming sensations as they talked, but the temptation was far too great to resist. So she looked at Jordan several times from head to toe. And it was obvious that she was gawking, so Jordan unplugged the iron and walked to the bed to laid beside Keleya.

Without thought or hesitation, Keleya placed her hand on Jordan's waist and ran her fingers across her toned stomach as a subtle cue to come closer. When she did so, Keleya pulled her closer, snugly between her legs as they kissed. Jordan slowly kissed her smooth neck and soft lips as Keleya caressed her strong back. After all, Jordan wanted her to. She wanted Keleya's hands to touch wherever they could reach. She needed her to get a good sample of what she was missing. But then she changed her mind. Jordan wanted Keleya to give in.

Jordan continued to kiss Keleya as she moved beside her. She stopped to lie back on the bed and look Keleya in the eyes. It was time for Keleya to make a decision. So Keleya mounted Jordan, placing the core of her womanhood firmly atop her hips. As Keleya removed her shirt, Jordan slowly ran her fingertips across her full breasts. She grasped Jordan's hand to caress her face. Then she leaned forward and kissed her deeply as Jordan positioned herself between her legs again. Jordan dropped her hand to unbutton Keleya's skinny jeans as she kissed along her neck and breasts. "Is this what you want?" she whispered.

Keleya stroked her locs and said, "Don't stop" as she

proceeded to remove her jeans. Just as Jordan shifted her weight to assist Keleya in sliding them off, someone knocked on the apartment door. She immediately stopped. "You expectin somebody?"

"No." Jordan got up and threw on a shirt. "I'll be right back." She stepped into the hallway and closed the door.

Keleya buttoned her pants and put on her shirt. She couldn't hear exactly what Jordan was saying, but she did hear the apartment door close. And the mystery person was now in the apartment conversing with Jordan. Jordan returned to the bedroom a few minutes later and sat beside Keleya. "Who is that?" she asked.

"My mom."

Keleya stared at Jordan with a blank expression. "Did you know she was comin over?"

"No," Jordan laughed. "Look, I know it's not funny and I promise I didn't know. She needs me to go to my grandmother's house for a while. I'll come to your apartment when I leave… is that okay?"

"Yeah."

"Come on," Jordan said as she stood from the bed. "Come meet her."

Keleya smiled. "Jordan…uh uhh. How the hell do you think it's gone look with me walkin out of your bedroom… with no shoes?"

Jordan laughed. "I told her you were here."

"Oh my god."

"She wants to meet you," Jordan said as she took hold of Keleya's hand.

Keleya didn't have a problem with meeting Jordan's mother. She just had a problem with the way she was meeting her, and it was damn near embarrassing. Keleya stood up and walked towards the door. Before they left the bedroom, Jordan gave her a hug for confidence, but Keleya pushed her away and walked into the hallway leading to the living room. She walked in and spoke to Jordan's mother. Her mother smiled, spoke back and introduced herself as Denise as Keleya sat on the love seat. While Jordan chatted with her mother, Keleya grew fidgety. She attempted to alleviate some of her uneasiness by texting her sister. However, what she really wanted to do was put on her sandals to feel more comfortable. But the shoes were between Jordan and Denise. So she just sat there thinking about how this woman looked nothing like she envisioned. She was tall, thin and very expressive when she talked. She reminded Keleya of Aunt Tink. Jordan left a few minutes later to get dressed. And now Keleya was both uncomfortable and alone. "It's nice to meet you Keleya," Denise said as she rummaged through her purse. "I've heard a lot of good things about you."

"It's nice to meet you too."

"Are you from Memphis?"

"Yes ma'am. I was born in Atlanta, but I'm from here."

"I was here until I was eighteen and then I had to go," Denise said and laughed. "What do you and Jordan have planned for today?"

"Mmm," Keleya paused. There was no way she could have this conversation without the sandals. So she got up, grabbed them and sat down to place them on her feet as she resumed her answer. "I don't know, we—"

Denise abruptly turned her head and covered her mouth as she laughed. "I'm sorry," she said. "I know ya'll are grown, but I can't help but laugh."

Keleya smiled for a second, but at this point she was highly embarrassed. Jordan's mother had all but admitted that she was aware that her surprise visit was dually a disruption.

Denise finally stopped laughing to say, "I'm sorry. Go ahead. What do you have planned for today?"

"We don't have anything planned. And I really don't wanna go anywhere because I've worked all week."

"Mmm hmm. I know what you mean," Denise commented as her cell phone rang. She said excuse me and took the call. Keleya was profoundly relieved when Denise stepped outside to continue the conversation.

When she exited, Keleya grabbed her purse and walked to Jordan's bedroom to say goodbye. "Call me when you leave."

"What you about to do?" Jordan asked as she walked with Keleya to the front door.

"I'm going to get my niece for a while." When they reached the door, Jordan stepped forward and kissed Keleya, but she eventually pulled away.

"What? You can't kiss you now?"

"Yo momma is outside the door," Keleya responded. She opened the apartment door and walked outside, waving goodbye to Denise as Jordan walked with her to the car.

By the time Jordan called, it was late in the evening. Keleya had picked up her niece and sister for lunch and an afternoon in the park, went shopping, dropped Nkosazana off, and driven home to play games and eat dinner with her niece. The two of them were now stretched out under a blanket. "What you doing?" Jordan asked.

"Watchin a movie with Nya."

"I didn't know my mom would be gone that long."

"J, it's fine."

"You not mad cause it took me so long to get back with you are you?"

"No, I'm not."

"Well I am."

"Why?"

"Because…shit, I was lookin forward to finishin what we started earlier."

Keleya laughed. Janya was bothered by their conversation, so she turned around and said, "I can't hear."

"Uhh! Attitude!" Keleya responded. She got up and walked to her bedroom.

"What did she say?" Jordan asked.

"That I was too loud."

"If I come over tomorrow, are we going to, you know, continue?"

Keleya laughed. "You missed your opportunity, so move on girl."

"Keleya, I'm serious. Why you playin?"

Keleya laughed again. "Jordan…look. I'm open to it…so when it happens it happens. Okay?" Jordan was on the phone, but she didn't respond. "You listenin to me?"

"Yeah…you're open to it now. You had me waitin this long, so we'll see."

Keleya smiled and sat on the oversized ottoman at the foot of her bed. She had reservations about asking the following question, but she asked anyway. "What did your momma say about me when I left?"

"What?"

"You heard me."

"Nothin."

"I don't believe that," Keleya stated. "Tell me what she said…was it bad?"

Jordan laughed and said, "No."

"So she did say somethin. Just tell me."

After a few seconds, Jordan spoke. "She said you were kind of top heavy."

Keleya burst into laughter and almost rolled onto the floor. "What else did she say?"

"She asked if you had any kids."

"What! Why would she ask that?"

"Because my last girlfriend had two…and they didn't like each other."

"Mmm…you didn't tell me she had children."

"Well she did. What you doing tomorrow?"

"Going over my momma house for a while. Tomorrow is her birthday."

"Ah for real?"

"Yeah…but I wanna see you. I want you to come over when I get home"

I talked to Jordan for a few more minutes and went back into the living room with Janya. I lay with her thinking about why I was so worried of what Jordan's mother thought about me. And I had to be honest with myself. The only reason I felt this way is because of Kris' mother. She always seemed as if she didn't want me around or didn't want to hear anything about me. I knew it didn't have anything to do with me in particular, but what she did and didn't do still affected me. She didn't care for our relationship and never came to terms with the fact that her daughter was lesbian and in love with me…a woman.

August 8th

KELEYA WAS HAVING a great morning. She awoke to sunshine and the smile of her niece. After eating breakfast, Keleya asked Janya what kind of gift she'd like to get for her grandmother. Janya decided her gift would be a homemade birthday cake. So they went to the grocery store and spent the remainder of the morning baking and decorating a two-layer chocolate cake.

That afternoon, Keleya enjoyed the company of her family. For Rita's fifty-third birthday, Keleya, her sisters and their children, as well as three of Rita's closest friends, celebrated by cooking a big meal and showering Rita with presents. When the gathering wound down, Keleya went into the kitchen with her sister to clean up and put away leftover food. "What you bout to do Leya?" Nkosazana asked.

"Going home to spend time with Jordan."

"So…ya'll serious? Ya'll together now?"

"Yes, I thought that was obvious."

"It is. I just didn't know the extent of it." Nkosazana stopped washing dishes. She dried her hands and turned around to face her sister. "Leya…you think this is somethin you should be doing right now? You were with Kris four years and now you in another relationship less than a year later… I know we done had our issues with this in the past and I know I ain't the one to be givin nobody advice on who they wanna be with, but I love you. You my little sister and I don't wanna see you hurt again…I'm just tryin to look out for you the way that you look out for me."

Keleya looked at Nkosazana and was immensely drawn to the tone of her voice. Something about it resonated in her heart. She could hear the part of her sister that she hadn't heard in a long time. This was the Nkosazana that protected her as a child. "Thanks Zana. I hear what you sayin, but I can't let Kris stop me from being with somebody else. I damn for sure ain't stopped her from doing what she do. Sometimes I don't know if I should feel this way about Jordan, but I know she feels the same way about me. So…"

"Well…I don't know what to say…I just want you to be happy."

Keleya talked with her sister for the next half hour. Then she left her mother's house and called Jordan to let her know that she was on the way home. And because it was a sweltering hot and humid Memphis day, she immediately took a shower. Less than an hour later, she unlocked the door so Jordan could walk directly into the apartment. When she entered, Keleya was sitting, facing the doorway. "What's in your hand?"

"This was at the door," Jordan replied. She sat beside Keleya and handed her a clear CD case. Keleya read the label on the disk. *Memphis Chix by Dréa and Lil' Vet*. "You know who they are?"

"Dréa is my ex's cousin. I don't know why she brought this over here." Keleya threw the CD onto the coffee table.

Jordan picked up the CD and said, "I wanna hear it."

"Go ahead." Jordan stood and put the CD in the DVD

player. The single began with Dréa and her rap mate giving shout-outs over the track. Keleya tuned out when she received a text from Kris.

U at home?
No. Why?
U know if Dréa left a cd over there?

Keleya decided not to text back and began to listen to the lyrics of the duet.

The neighbors know my name
She call me Dréa Hussein
Cause I be terrorizin that thang
And she be going insane
She flow like a flood
Got a tongue like a hurricane
Booty bounce like a quake
Bring yank like a tsunami mane

"Jordan cut that shit off."
"It wasn't that bad."
"I didn't say it was. I just don't wanna hear it."
Jordan stopped the CD and changed the subject. "Did you enjoy yourself today?"
"Yeah. We had a good time. We played Spades and cooked and hung out…actually, I cooked because my sisters can't cook worth a damn. But my momma was really happy…and I like to see her that way because I didn't see it all the time growing up. I mean we had good times, you know, but she didn't start to enjoy life again til I was in my twenties." As Jordan asked her next question, Keleya received another text. She knew the text was from Kris and for that reason she didn't read it.

She continued to talk to Jordan for the next hour, but in that length of time, Kris sent three additional messages.

"Who is that blowin up your phone?" Jordan asked. Keleya sat up to finally check the texts. Kris wanted to know if she'd arrived home. If so, she would come by to retrieve the CD. This time, Keleya sent a text back.

Why r u trying to get something that she left at MY APARTMENT? And why the hell did she bring it over here anyway?
R u at home?
U can get it tomorrow!
I'm on my way over there.
Do NOT come over here!!!
I just left.

Keleya stood up to get the CD from the player. "What's going on?" Jordan asked.

Keleya sighed heavily. "Kris is comin to get this."

"Right now?"

"Yeah. She's at her girlfriend's house. She lives back there," Keleya motioned.

"You mean in these apartments?"

"Yeah."

"Wait a minute. Your ex lives over here?"

"No, the girl that she's fuckin with lives over here," Keleya clarified. She didn't explain the who or why because Kris was calling. She answered the phone in a voice that blatantly announced that she was not happy with Kris' actions.

"I'm outside," Kris stated.

Keleya ended the call and looked at Jordan. "I'll be right back. Please don't come outside."

Jordan looked at Keleya for a few seconds. "I didn't plan on it."

Keleya went outside and walked up to Kris who was standing by the car. "And why the hell could you not wait til tomorrow to get this?"

Kris snatched the CD and threw it in the driver seat. "She shouldn't have brought it over here."

"Duh! But she did. And you didn't have to keep textin me to get it back."

"All I wanted you to do is what you did," Kris responded. "You didn't have to make me wait for almost two hours."

"Make you wait! Kris, I'm busy. You're the one askin me for somethin…anyway, it's too damn muggy out here to be foolin with you. Bye."

"Oh, okay. You in there with your girl, you can't give me two fuckin seconds of your time?"

In the midst of their ongoing exchange, neither Keleya nor Kris saw Soria turn the corner and walk towards them. "Kris!" Soria called out. Both Keleya and Kris looked in her direction.

"Man…get in the car," Kris directed as Soria drew closer.

"Why the fuck you over here?" Soria shouted. When Soria approached them, Keleya saw that she was drunk. And she was not down for the drama that Kris' new bitch was about to start, so she turned around to walk away.

"Hold on," Kris pleaded as she took hold of Keleya's arm. Without notice, Soria stepped forward and thrust Keleya's arm away. Keleya felt acrylic nails cut through her flesh from elbow to wrist. And she was *shocked*. Her reflex was to turn around and push Soria. So that is exactly what she did. And when Soria called her out of her name, Keleya lashed out. She redirected her frustrations for Kris by stepping to Soria, grabbing her by the collar and pushing her into the car. Kris tried to pull Keleya away while yelling at Soria to get in the car.

At some point, Jordan heard the altercation and opened the door. She ran to the car and grabbed Keleya. When she noticed that Jordan was restraining her, she came to her senses. Keleya pushed Jordan away and grasped her arm in pain as she walked into the apartment. She went straight to her bedroom and locked the door.

Keleya sat on the bed upset and embarrassed. She was embarrassed by the display, mostly because Jordan witnessed some of it. She replayed the last few minutes in her head, and it wasn't until that moment she realized that Soria could not defend herself because of her intoxication. She recalled strangling Soria and Kris begging for her to let go. Just as she was about to stand, she heard Jordan approach the bedroom door. "Keleya...can you open the door?" Jordan asked, but Keleya didn't move. "Kelee-baby."

"Jordan...give me a minute, okay?" Keleya stood from the bed and walked into the bathroom. She wet a face towel and wiped the blood from her right arm. Then she got another towel and washed her face. She exited the bathroom and opened the door for Jordan. Jordan stepped in and demanded to see her arm. When she extended her arm to reveal long lines of welts and scratches, she noticed a smudge of blood on Jordan's shirt.

"Does it hurt?" Jordan asked.

Keleya just looked at Jordan. 'Duh!' she thought. "Burns like hell." Jordan let go of her wrist. "I'm sorry Jordan," she said as her anger settled. "I didn't know that was going to happen."

"It's okay," Jordan said as she stepped forward and hugged Keleya. "You didn't want it to." After stroking her back, Jordan gently placed her hands on Keleya's face and kissed her forehead. She tried to console her by saying, "It's okay baby," but she felt kissing her lips would do it better.

Keleya allowed each kiss to remove a layer of her physical and emotional pain. Jordan made her feel comforted and desired at the same time. She felt the best way to show appreciation for Jordan's warmth and concern was to stop making her wait. So to reassure Jordan that there would be no backing down on her part, she led Jordan to the bed. After Jordan sat down, Keleya stepped between her legs and slowly undressed. As she unveiled her shapely figure, Jordan playfully ran the tips of her fingers across her breasts and the palms of her hands around her hips. Jordan touched Keleya as if this was the first time she'd caressed a woman, but there was a grave maturity in the placement and pace. And her touch alone was fulfilling. Keleya was now so intrigued to know what it would feel like for Jordan to have her completely that she said damn the four play. She straddled Jordan's lap and kissed her fiercely. Jordan took hold of her hips and moved to the middle of the bed, placing Keleya on her back and spreading her legs. She ran her hand up Keleya's leg until she reached her ultra smooth inner thigh. There was absolutely no need for introductions, so Keleya took Jordan's hand and invited her in. And Jordan didn't leave until they were both fully satisfied.

Keleya laid her head on Jordan's shoulder and massaged her stomach and waist for almost thirty minutes. And neither said a word. Instead, they laid there basking in brown skin, the smell of pleasure and the glory of orgasms. Her climax was long awaited so Keleya held onto the feeling as long as she could. Eventually, she propped herself up and looked in Jordan's eyes. "J, I don't want you to think that the only reason I had sex with you is because of what happened tonight."

Jordan rubbed Keleya's face. "I don't. To be honest… I don't want you to feel like I took advantage of the situation."

"I don't feel that way. We both wanted this."

I was glad that we were both clear on how we perceived each other's intentions. I told Jordan about Dréa and Soria, and then we talked and fell asleep. Jordan woke up around 4:00 and left. I was disappointed by her departure even though I knew we both had to go to work in a few hours. But going to work today wouldn't be so bad...I'd have something great to think about all day.

September 18th

INTIMACY ADDS DIMENSION to relationships. And that's exactly what it did for Keleya and Jordan. They had a passion for each other's company, which began to form an emotional dependency. Keleya could now say that she was in a relationship—a connection built on friendship and mutuality.

Keleya woke up at 6:00 in the morning. It was the weekend and still dark outside, so she had the option of falling asleep again. However, she put on a UT t–shit and a pair of jeans and went to Kroger. There was something enjoyable about being one of the only shoppers in the grocery store, so she bought more than anticipated. As she pushed a loaded cart through the exit doors, an employee beckoned her attention. "Ay shawty, you need some help?" asked a young stud before lighting a cigarette.

Keleya stopped to get keys from her purse and to take a look at this woman. Her name badge read "Ty" and she couldn't have been any older than twenty. "No, but thank you," Keleya replied.

"What you doing up so early? You gettin breakfast for yo man?"

"My man?" Keleya said as she walked away. 'Guess you can't spot fam,' she thought.

"If you ain't got a man and you eatin alone, I can give you some company," Ty smiled as she walked with Keleya.

"Are you not at work?"

Before Ty answered, a coworker called her name. "I done seen you in here before, so I'll see you later Miss Lady," Ty smiled as she turned and walked away.

Keleya returned home and made three trips from the car to the dining room floor to carry groceries and toiletries inside. But before placing food in the refrigerator, she decided to clean the whole thing. In the middle of washing the vegetable drawer, she received a call from Jordan. Given that it was early morning, she wondered if the call bore bad news. She answered the phone reluctant to say hello. "Did I wake you up?" Jordan asked.

"No. What's going on?" Keleya asked with haste.

"Come open the door for me. I'm outside."

Keleya opened the apartment door and blocked Jordan's entry. "What? Why you lookin at me like that?" Jordan asked.

"Because it's not even 8:00 on a Saturday morning and you're up...and here. Can I get an explanation?"

"Damn baby, can you let me in first?" Keleya took two steps back. "I just left work. I was on call."

"What happened?"

As Jordan responded, Keleya realized the refrigerator door was still open. She walked into the kitchen to continue cleaning as Jordan followed telling her story. "...got there around 6:30 and went straight to the conference room because they'd already removed the girls from the milieu. When I walked in, the shift worker walked out and I sat down with the girls—one ten and one eleven. I had already read the shift summary. But like I told you before, when I go into situations like this, nobody gives me in-depth details about the incident cause I want to hear the girls' side of the story before I process with staff or other counselors. Everybody don't do it like that, but you know I do me. So, I started with the younger one and asked her to explain to me what happened, and then I listened to the other girl. To make a long story short, they got into a fight this morning over a Rihanna CD."

"Why were they up so early in the morning?"

"Meds. They never went to sleep. But that's an issue in itself. So…at some point in this fight, they broke the CD. And then the ten-year-old picked up a piece of the CD—which you know was sharp—and tried to stab the eleven-year-old. Eventually a staff person caught wind of it, broke up the fight and called me at 6:00."

Keleya didn't have words to say. Her only expression was, "Mmm mm."

Keleya continued to talk to Jordan as she completed the cleaning and placed the food into the refrigerator. When that was done, she washed her hands and looked at Jordan who was sitting atop the island. She stepped over and stood between her girlfriend's legs with a smile. "What?" Jordan asked.

Keleya rubbed her hands along Jordan's legs. "You look hell of good today Jordan Alexander."

Jordan smiled and said, "No."

"What you sayin no for? I didn't ask you anything."

"Cause you on my top. I know what you doing."

"And what is that?"

Jordan took hold of Keleya's hands. "It ain't happenin."

Keleya took her hands back and began to unbutton Jordan's plaid shirt. But Jordan stopped her at the second opening. "Leya, what the hell?" she laughed. "Remember the other day when I wanted to have sex but you pushed me away and pretty much told me to leave you the hell alone cause you were busy?"

Keleya laughed. "I like sex in the morning."

"Okay, for ignorin me, I'm really not givin you any."

Keleya smiled and kissed Jordan's neck. She could hear and feel the change in Jordan's breathing patterns—therefore her actions would ultimately speak louder than her words. She placed Jordan's hands on her hips to entice her even more and whispered, "Let's go to my room" as she rolled her hips. Now that Jordan was warmed up, Keleya knew she would be more than willing to follow any command. So she pulled Jordan from the island and undressed her a bit more before leading her to the bedroom. She placed her arms around Jordan's neck. "Kiss me," she whispered.

As Jordan's hands fell from Keleya's back to the curves of her cheeks, they slowly kissed. Being next to Jordan was so seductive that Keleya changed her mind about the location and removed her t-shirt. After Jordan removed everything else, she helped lift Keleya onto the island. Keleya laid back and opened her legs so that Jordan could quickly access the goodness. Jordan's technique was so good that Keleya simultaneously caressed and forcefully pulled her locs. She thought Jordan would eventually make her stop, but it turned Jordan on—in return pleasuring Keleya even more. But after a while, Keleya grew greedy. She placed her hand on Jordan's face and sat up. She pulled Jordan towards her and kissed her shiny lips. "Let's go," she demanded.

Once in the bedroom, Keleya fully undressed Jordan. She instructed Jordan to lay down so that part two could begin with a passionate trib. Once the morning engagement was over, Jordan rest her head on Keleya's stomach as they held hands and talked. "Are you nervous about the grant? I been meanin to ask you that."

"No," Keleya replied. "But I can't stand the wait."

"I think you'll get it Kelee...I know you will. You wrote a solid proposal and I know this is somethin you'll be good at.

Plus, the program is needed in this city…but I can't lie Keleya, you surprised me."

"Surprised you?"

"Yeah. I wasn't surprised by like the quality of it because you're hella smart, so that's what I expected. I was kind of taken aback cause you took the idea and ran with it. You decided it was somethin that you wanted so you put a lot of work into it in a short amount of time…that's admirable."

"Thanks baby…you know, I told my momma and sister what I was doing, or would be doing, the other day and they both gave me a dumb ass look. They really didn't understand what I'd do if I got the funding. The only thing my momma asked is if I'd quit my job and that shit offended me so I ended the conversation…but, it wasn't a conversation cause I was the only one talkin about it. And then I guess Zana just completely ignored my reaction because she turned around and asked me if that meant I could give her a job." Jordan laughed. "That shit pissed me off so I got up and left."

"Hey…that's your fam."

Keleya was going to continue, but her phone rang. Jordan got up to get the cell phone from the nightstand. "Who is it?" Keleya asked.

"It say's Eric dos Santos." After Jordan handed her the phone, Keleya placed the call on speaker so that Jordan could hear the ensuing dialogue.

"Hello," Keleya answered unenthusiastically.

"Keleya. How you doing? This is your father."

"I know…how are you?"

"I'm good…real good…I just…I just wanted to call and talk to you cause I ain't heard from you in almost a year."

"I know. I've been here."

After a moment of silence, Eric continued. "I wanted to make sure you were okay…maybe we can get together next month around Thanksgiving."

"Okay…just let me know when."

"Alright…tell your mother I said hello."

"I will."

"Alright then. I'll call you soon."

Keleya ended the call, dropped her phone on the bed and looked at Jordan. "As you could hear, that was my biological father."

"dos Santos?" Jordan questioned.

"I think his grandparents were Afro–Brazilian."

"Mmm…baby, I don't mean to sound judgmental, but did you have to be so rude?"

Keleya rolled her eyes and got out the bed to get a shirt from the dresser. "He always does this shit where he just calls me out the blue. And he ain't gone call to get together for no fuckin Thanksgiving…you don't understand," Keleya commented as she sat down.

Jordan placed her hand on Keleya's back. "I can…come here baby."

Although slightly upset, Keleya lay beside Jordan. As Jordan rubbed her arm, she began to relax. When her normal temperament returned, she shared with Jordan the root of her resentment. "I used to spend a lot time with him. I would stay with him for a month every summer and a week or two during Christmas break. The summer between fifth and sixth grade I went and stayed with him and his wife and her sons. One was a year older than me and the other one was about a year and half older than his brother.

"One day, me and the younger brother were outside behind the shed throwing sticks into the neighbor's yard…the next thing I knew the older brother came around the corner and grabbed me from behind while the other one pulled my pants and underwear down. He pulled his down too but Eric showed up and they ran away. I pulled my clothes up and stood there because I didn't know what to do…I think it took him a minute to process everything because he grabbed me and pushed me into the shed. He was holdin me so tight that he left a bruise on my arm…I didn't hear a word he said, cause shit, I was damn near traumatized…but eventually he let go and said get yo ass in the house. I went in and locked myself in the room.

"When his wife got home, she pried the door open and asked her husband what was wrong with me. He said he didn't know and that it didn't matter cause I was going home the next day anyway. And when he drove me home, he didn't say shit to me til he dropped me off. And the only reason he said somethin then was because my momma was standin there… of course she was excited to see me and wanted to know how my visit was. I lied and told her it was fine, but as soon as I had the opportunity to tell Zana what happened I did…at that point in my life, she was my best friend…she was the one who took care of me and she told me not to worry about it because I would never have to go back again.

"So…sixth grade started and Christmas break came and my momma made plans for me to leave. I remember her gettin off the phone and tellin me that Eric would pick me up that weekend. So Zana told me to wait til the day before I was supposed to leave and say that I'd started my period. I was eleven! Faking my period was worse than going back to Little Rock—and you can imagine what it was like when I did actually start my cycle and had to keep it to myself.

"But anyway, at the end of the day, I didn't have any other options. I thought about tellin my momma why I didn't wanna go back, but she was dead set on shipping her children out the house for a few days. And it's sad to say, but I knew my eleven-year-old allegation wouldn't be enough to convince a woman with a habit to let me stay home. So I went ahead and told her that I'd started my period. So instead of makin me go to stay with him, I went to my grandma's house.

"And that was the last time I stayed with him. My momma would make me call him and he came here a few times, but she never really pressed the issue. And once I graduated from high school that was it for me. I was done with him. He's never brought up what happened or apologized for what he did. So…I don't call him. He calls me."

After I was done with the history behind why I have no relationship with my father, we talked about why Eric may have responded in the manner that he did. Jordan asked if my experience that summer might have influenced my sexual orientation. I gave her a firm and adamant hell no and explained that my same sex preference has existed for as long as I can remember—which then led me into a speech about the many times people have tried to rationalize for me why I'm gay. Jordan shared her experiences with people in and outside of her family projecting their "gay theories" upon her and then we talked about a few other things that happened to us in our childhoods. I didn't mean to tell Jordan most of what I did, but at the same time, I didn't have a problem disclosing it. I just didn't think it would be under these circumstances…I guess there's something about sex and intimacy that makes me open and…vulnerable.

October 7th

THE ARRIVAL OF milder weather influenced Keleya to purchase a six-month membership to a nearby fitness center. Even though she hated to work out in a facility, she was dedicated to her routine. She left work and went directly to the gym for an hour run. During the workout she'd received a call from Donyelle but decided not to return it until arriving home and completing a few tasks. "Hey DD," Keleya greeted.

"Hey. What you doing?"

"Nothin now. I was at the gym when you called. You feelin any better?"

"I'm better…it still hurts, but I ain't takin no more of them pain killers cause they make me go to sleep."

"You not there by yourself are you? Where is Meka?"

"Sittin right here beside me."

"Oh. Tell her I said hey."

After speaking on Keleya's behalf, Donyelle asked, "Where Jordan at?"

"In Philly."

"So that's why you called me back today? Cause she's out of town?"

Keleya laughed. "DD, I always call you back."

"No you don't, but that's okay. I ain't mad about it…how

long she been gone?"

"Six days."

"You miss her?"

Keleya thought about her answer for a second. "Yeah, a little bit."

"Why? Because you want some?"

Keleya laughed. "Girl, I'm for real. I do miss her...and that...but I'll see her Sunday."

"Have you talked to her?"

"I talk to her everyday." As Keleya chatted with her cousin, the conversation shifted to include Meka, who wanted Keleya's opinion about dominance and strap usage in their relationship. After their semi-heated exchange, Keleya lounged for the rest of the evening.

• • •

Keleya went to work the next day as usual. Before leaving the office, she decided to spend the remainder of the day at home alone, treating herself to movies, music and artistry. She left work at 4:00 and went straight home to indulge. She'd already talked to everyone who could potentially call, including Jordan, so she didn't foresee any interruptions. But at 5:41, someone did just that. Keleya sat the jade pendant on the table and stood from the floor to peek through the blinds in order to see who rang the doorbell. There was a young Black man standing on the porch with flowers in his hands. She cracked the door a little and looked at him. "I have a gift for Ms. Smith," he said.

Since he was at the correct location, Keleya responded, "That's me." She received the bouquet of three-dozen yellow roses and said, "Thanks. Have a good day." Keleya shut the door and placed the roses on the dining room table. She of course knew who'd sent the roses, so she pulled the card from the large arrangement eager to read her message.

Even if you were taken from me, I'd find my way back to you because you're my sunshine Keleya.

XOXO Jordan

Oh my god! I couldn't even think of thoughts to express the way I felt. So I stood there for a moment because I was more than flattered, I was floored—not just because of the delivery of roses, yellow roses, but because Jordan read the book. She'd taken the time to read Sundiata. I grabbed my phone and called her. I had to thank her for the roses and I had to hear her voice because now I missed her...a lot.

October 10th

TODAY IS *THE* day—the day that ends nine days of waiting. Jordan's flight would arrive in Memphis at 4:40 that afternoon, but Keleya wouldn't see her until 8:00. Jordan would spend time with her family before Keleya came to the apartment. To ease the wait, Keleya went to her mother's house for a few hours since Nkosazana and Janya were there. When she walked in, her sister and mother were standing in the kitchen washing and seasoning split chicken breasts. "What you makin Momma?"

"Chicken and dumplings," Rita answered.

Because she didn't hear any sounds from her niece in the den—who was never completely quiet for more than a few seconds—Keleya asked her sister, "Where Janya at?"

"Next door at the candy lady," Nkosazana responded. Keleya immediately got up to unlock the storm door.

"Leya, do me a favor and call Stacy for me right quick," Rita requested before Keleya returned to her seat. Keleya had absolutely no desire to call her sister, but she grabbed the cordless phone off the countertop as if she would comply.

Fortunately, Janya came back in the nick of time, giving her aunt a valid diversion. "What you got in that bag Smurf?"

Janya was too focused on biting and removing polystyrene from the top of a green freeze cup to reply, so she poured the contents of the brown bag onto the tabletop. "You can have some if you want," she said after a moment. "I gotta lot of stuff."

"I see," Keleya noted. For $3, Janya had purchased a medium freeze cup, twenty Tootsie rolls, and fifteen cherry and banana Laffy Taffy's.

"You wanna see the book Granny got me?" Janya asked.

"Yeah. Where is it?" Keleya followed Janya into the den to see the book. After coloring a few pages with her niece, she returned to kitchen. "I brought ya'll some necklaces," she said as she pulled a bag from her purse.

"Thanks," Rita responded, "but we can only wear so much at one time Leya. You spend too much money on that stuff. I don't understand why you don't sell it."

"Momma…now you know I don't wanna sell my pieces."

"I know you don't *want* to, but if you gone spend $40 to make one necklace, why not sell it? If you sell it for $40— even though it can go for more than that cause you make good stuff—at least you get your money back."

Keleya was once again irritated by Rita's constant fixation on money. So she sat there with her arms crossed staring at her mother who then looked at her daughter. Rita saw by Keleya's body language that she was not buying it. When Rita turned around, Keleya glanced at her sister, who remained oddly silent in the matter. She quickly remembered why and reflected on the few times that Nkosazana had sold several of her pieces for personal gain. "If you don't want it, I'll give it to the folks work," Keleya said as she began to drop Janya's candy back into the bag.

"No…I didn't say that," Rita asserted. "You sent any to your grandmomma and Tink or Carolyn?"

"Mmm hmm. I do all the time."

Rita washed her hands and went into the den with Janya.

Nkosazana sat with her sister, opening the bag of necklaces to neatly spread all five on the tabletop as they talked. "Where is Jordan?" Nkosazana asked.

Keleya slapped her hand on the glass. "Why is it that every time I talk to somebody they ask me where she at?"

"Leya, don't play. You know ya'll always together."

"No we not. We spend time apart."

"When? When ya'll at work?"

Keleya glanced at the floor. She knew her sister was mostly right. "She been gone all week. But she comin back today, and I'm going to see her tonight," Keleya explained while snapping and performing a short celebration dance.

Nkosazana smiled and shook her head. "When the last time you talked to Kris?"

"Do you not see me over here radiating about the fact that my baby is comin home."

Nkosazana placed her hand on her hip and said, "Answer the damn question."

"Not since August lady."

"Mmm mm. Ya'll need to stop. Just cause ya'll ain't together don't mean ya'll can't be friends. Is it that bad?" Nkosazana asked, but Keleya didn't answer the question. She changed the subject and continued to chat with Nkosazana before going home to shower.

Keleya left for Jordan's apartment a few minutes before 8:00 and called to announce her arrival upon entering the parking lot of the building. She got out of the car holding one of the long stemmed yellow roses. Jordan was standing in the doorway waiting for her to appear. But when Keleya got to door, she wasn't sure what she noticed first—the fact the Jordan was high as hell or the smell of weed hitting her in the face. Whatever the case, when she stepped into the apartment Jordan walked away. Keleya shut the door and stood there for a second. This was definitely not the welcome she anticipated. And when she walked over to the couch, Jordan didn't move. Instead, she sat there with her elbows on her legs and a blunt in her hand. Keleya knew something was seriously wrong because this was a facet of Jordan's life that she kept to herself, even within their relationship. But now, she had shamelessly unmasked.

Jordan eventually sat the blunt in an ashtray and took Keleya's hand. "Sit down Kelee." Keleya sat beside Jordan and moved an almost empty glass of brown liquor next to the ashtray to place her purse and the rose on the table. "You brought that for me?" Jordan asked with a smile. Keleya looked at her with disappointment. "What's wrong?"

"I should be askin you that," Keleya snapped. Jordan sighed, leaned back and stared at the ceiling. "Jordan what's wrong with you?"

Because of her delayed responses, it took Jordan a few seconds to answer. "I got off the plane...in the car with my momma and she took me straight to the hospital...she didn't even tell me my grandma was admitted yesterday...I can't deal with this...I can't deal with people I love being sick...or death." Jordan paused for a while and then rubbed her eyes. "Shit...I'm sorry Kelee-baby...it's been over a week since we seen each other and...I fucked it up for you."

Right! Keleya was fucking upset! But she checked herself and instantly pushed aside her feelings to comfort Jordan. She stood to sit in Jordan's lap, wrapping her arms around her tightly and resting her head on her chest. "What's her condition?"

"She's responsive," Jordan replied slowly. "But she's fighting an infection...I don't know. I just know I'm stressed as hell and it's gettin to me...I didn't move down here to watch her die."

"Don't stress out about it. I know you have a lot of things

on your plate, but you shouldn't worry about this because I think she'll be okay...I really do," Keleya said before kissing Jordan's face. She wanted to be reassuring and supportive, but she also had to be honest. "Baby," Keleya continued as she rubbed Jordan's locs, "you gotta find a better way to deal with it...you need to find a way that's not illegal." Jordan gave a half smile. "Well...I take that back because legalities don't have shit to do with it. I just want you to find a way to cope that's not doing more harm than good."

Jordan looked at me and gently touched the hairline of my neck. It was so fucking soothing that I kissed her...and I couldn't stop. I took our shirts off so that we could have more contact. And after I kissed her more, I unbuttoned her jeans. I slid off the couch onto my knees to remove everything below her waist, and then I brought her hips forward. Her brown skin was soft and smooth as normal, but cold. So I rubbed my hands up and down her legs as I rhythmically stroked her with my tongue. Sex was not the best substitute for a coping mechanism, but at that moment I felt anything was better than a depressant. I took her hand and placed it on my head so that she could feel me dive deeper. And as Jordan grew less tense, she became saturated with wet ecstasy. I knew it was selfish as hell to take advantage of her moment of weakness, but I didn't stop until she came twice over. Plus, there was something wholly erotic about the smell of weed over Burberry Touch. And I felt like we both needed to be close to each other...very close...so we were.

December 11th

IT HAD BEEN over ten weeks since Keleya submitted the proposal for the grant. She remained patient, but grew tired of the wait. She began to check the mailbox anxiously and daily. USPS delivered during the eleven o'clock hour. So as soon as noon struck, Keleya threw on a coat and headed outside. She walked to the mailbox with a strong feeling that a letter would be there. Regardless if the letter stated *thank you for your submission* or *congratulations*, she wasn't nervous about the outcome.

As fate would have it, the letter was there. She quickly walked back to the apartment and unlocked the door. She sat down, tore the seal of the envelope and scanned the message. Affirmative! She was awarded a $25,000 project grant effective January 1. Her instinct was to scream, but she was too overwhelmed to move. But eventually she had to get up and celebrate. She grabbed her keys and purse from the dining room table and jumped in the car. She had to personally show Jordan the good news.

After parking beside Jordan's SUV, Keleya got out the car with letter in hand and proceeded to the steps at the front of the building. As she approached the end of the long and wide wrap around porch, she could hear voices. However, she didn't think anything of it. But as soon as she turned the corner that led to the entrance of Jordan's apartment, she immediately took a step back to hide her presence. She stood on the opposite side of the brick wall in pure disbelief because Jordan was holding and kissing another woman.

Keleya was unsure how to proceed. So she stood frozen, eavesdropping on the conversation. From what she could hear through the distraction of traffic on the neighboring thoroughfare, Jordan was kissing this woman goodbye. And upon catching the distinct sound of this woman's voice, Keleya realized she was Renée—the coworker.

Keleya walked away infuriated. But soon as she put her foot on the first step that led to the parking lot, she stopped. Something made her think about Veda and she felt foolish for her lack of action that night. Keleya turned around ready to regulate, but she thought about Kris and stopped. So much pain came over her body that she finally went down the stairs. Keleya opened the car door and noticed that she was still holding the funding letter. She turned around to face Jordan's car and instantly tasted revenge. However, she took a deep breath and walked to the front of the SUV to place the letter under the driver's side windshield wiper. She figured Jordan might as well have the letter because she'd just stripped her of all joy.

Keleya drove directly home. She stepped into her apartment, locked the door and sat on the couch. She dropped her purse on the floor and cut on the TV on. She wrapped herself in a blanket all afternoon and well into the evening. But around 8:30, she became tired of her depressive state, so she got up and called JaCola. "Cola you at home?" she asked with melancholy in her voice.

"Yeah. What's wrong with you?"

"You mind if I come over?"

"You know I don't. What's wrong?"

"I need to…" Keleya paused. She longed for a listening ear, but didn't want JaCola to feel as if she were being used in any way.

"Leya just get in the car and leave."

When Keleya walked into their apartment, Maleek was sitting on the living room floor wearing Spiderman pajamas and playing with blocks. JaCola directed Keleya to follow her into the bedroom so they could talk in private. Keleya walked into the room and sat in the recliner. She didn't want to replay the day's occurrence, but she knew JaCola was waiting on explanation for her presence and noncharacteristic mood. "What happened Leya? Ya'll got into an argument?"

Keleya shook her head no. "I got the grant."

"Are you serious!" JaCola shouted. "I knew you would get it. Did you get the full amount?"

"Yep…$25,000," Keleya said void of enthusiasm.

"Why am I the only one happy about it?" JaCola noted. Keleya looked away, staring off into the distance before dropping her head. "Are you okay?"

"Barely," Keleya stated through a cracking voice. She held back wavering emotions and looked at JaCola again. "As soon as I got the letter I left and went to see Jordan. Her apartment is on the side of the building, so you walk down this long porch and then turn…when I turned the corner she was standing outside kissing Renée."

"What? You mean the Renée my sister know? The one they work with?" JaCola shouted.

"Yeah," Keleya said softly as she placed her face in her hands and rubbed her eyes.

"Are you sure? I mean…I know it was another woman, but you sure it was Renée? I can't believe that shit!"

"Well believe it."

"I should call Angie right now," JaCola exclaimed as she stood from the bed.

"Please don't Cola. Sit down."

"Are you *sure* it was Renée?"

"Yes Cola! I've met her and personally talked to her."

"That's some low down dirty shit...what did Jordan do when she saw you?" JaCola asked as she sat down.

"She didn't see me...neither one of them did."

"She didn't see you? How'd that happen?"

"They were too fuckin consumed with each other sayin goodbye and shit to notice me," Keleya said frustrated. She paused to take a moment to lessen her temper. "When I saw them I left."

"You left? Your girlfriend was with Renée and you left!" JaCola said before rolling her eyes. "Have you talked to her?"

"Not since last night...and for all I know she could have been with her then...but...I didn't have it in me to do or say anything."

"So she ain't called or text you all day?"

"No."

"Ya'll talk everyday so why wouldn't she call you? Cause you said she didn't see you."

"Because she knows that I know."

"How is that?"

"I left the letter on her windshield."

"The letter you got in the mail today?"

"Yeah."

"Why would you..." JaCola stopped and thought about it for a second. "Oh...damn...that's fucked up...I don't know what to say." After sitting in silence for a moment, JaCola said, "I'll be right back." She left the room to check on Maleek and returned with a cup of apple juice. "What you gone do?"

Keleya stared at the bed. "I don't know...nothin."

"Damn, I thought ya'll leslies didn't have this problem," JaCola joked to lighten the mood.

"Shut up!" Keleya smiled.

JaCola suggested that I contact Jordan to at least express the way I felt—especially given the fact that Jordan knows what happened in my last relationship. But I'll be damned if I call her! Besides, I don't have to because I'm pretty sure she is going to call me...I know she will. The problem is that I really don't know if I want to talk to Jordan. The only thing I'm sure about is the way I feel right now...and I didn't feel this bad when my relationship ended with Kris.

December 15th

TODAY MADE DAY number four. Keleya began to wonder if Jordan would altogether avoid the rift in their relationship. But she held her ground. She was *not* contacting Jordan. When Keleya left work, she went to a small crafts shop to assess their inventory. While at checkout, she received a text from Jordan. *I get off at 6:30. Will you be at home? We need to talk.* In the last forty-eight hours, Keleya decided that she did indeed want to talk with Jordan. But now, she was unsure if she should follow through with the decision. However, she text back, *Yes.*

Keleya got to her apartment a few minutes before 6:00. Within the next hour, Jordan would be in her space again. She went into the kitchen and warmed up leftover spaghetti as she thought about how quickly an environment could change and how someone could go from friend to foe in a moment's time.

Jordan knocked on the door at 6:52. Keleya unlocked and pulled the door slightly open, but she didn't welcome Jordan in. As she walked to the far end of the sectional, Jordan stepped inside and shut the door, but she didn't leave the entryway. She placed her hands in her pockets and said, "Hey."

Keleya looked at Jordan, but there was no way she could greet someone that she simultaneously cared for and despised. "Why did you wait to contact me?"

Jordan dropped her head and looked up again. "Because I know that I hurt you and that you'd need some time."

"You decided it would be best for me to wait four days?"

"Okay, I shouldn't speak for you. But I apologize for hurting you."

"You're not apologetic for anything else?" Keleya asked next, but Jordan didn't answer. Keleya looked away and shook her head. "So when did you start sleepin with her? Before Hard Rock or after?"

After a disheartening silence, Jordan answered, "Before."

Keleya looked at the floor and inhaled deeply. It took everything in her power to fight back a juggernaut of anger. "You know *exactly* what my ex did to me…you know. And you turn around and do the same thing behind my back for months knowing how much trust I put in you."

"Keleya why you so fuckin self–righteous?" Jordan immediately countered. "Shit…did I step to you about Veda?"

"Excuse me!" Keleya thought they would have an amicable exchange, but that assumption was now thrown out the window. "Jordan, you got some muthafuckin nerve steppin into my apartment callin me self–righteous and accusin me of somethin I didn't do! And when the hell did you start going through my texts? She kissed me. That was it! And contrary to what you assume, I haven't given her the time of day since. And let's not forget, *I'm* the one who caught you with the woman you told me to go to for advice. The woman that you've been fuckin this whole damn relationship. And now you wanna throw labels and shit! Cause if you wanna take it there, let me know and I'll start."

Jordan sighed. "Yo, I didn't come over here to argue with you. I came to be honest and say I'm sorry. But damn, how the fuck you think I feel? I didn't wanna lie to you. I—"

"But you did!" Keleya interrupted. "And you did it in the most *disrespectful* way."

"You're right. I should have been honest with you from jump and ended my friends with benefits status with Renée. But...I need you to understand that...Keleya it's hard to be in a position where you're falling in love with a woman whose heart belongs to someone else. And I don't give a damn what you say, I *was* your fuckin rebound. If you could be with your ex— you know, the one whose name is tattooed on your waist—you would be. You made that shit clear in so many words from day one...I stayed and pursued this relationship with you because I was feeling you. I fooled myself into believin that you would get over her and start to feel the same way about me. But you didn't! So why the hell did you think I would give you everything if you couldn't do the same for me?"

Keleya propped her arm on the sectional to rest her head for a moment. "Jordan...you know I'm not unreasonable to the point that I can't understand where you're comin from. And...I partially agree with some of what you said." She paused to look at Jordan who was staring into the kitchen. "But are you seriously going to stand there and justify what you were doing and use it to downplay the way I feel about you?"

"The way you feel about me? Whatever," Jordan scoffed. "You were enjoying yourself."

Keleya rolled her eyes and peered out the window. "Enjoying myself? Okay. Yeah. I enjoy meeting a woman and spendin time with her, gettin to know her, initiating a relationship with her, *building* a relationship with her, being intimate with her *and* another woman. So yes! I guess I did enjoy every fuckin moment of that shit."

"Look," Jordan said and exhaled. "I wish I could have done some things differently for your sake and mine...

but when you decide who and what you want, I'll be here." Jordan stepped forward, took the funding letter from her back pocket and placed it on the dining room table. She exited without saying a word.

I waited until Jordan drove away before I got up and locked the door. Then I went into my bedroom to get ready for work. When I got in bed, I lay there thinking about the things Jordan said. I tried to not let the fact that she was having a prolonged sexual relationship with Renée overshadow the reality of Kris still being an influence in my life. However, I couldn't let go. I was mad at Jordan, but the anger wasn't enough to instantly erase my feelings for her. Instead, I lay there burning inside because the woman I had a wonderful connection with was gone.

December 17th

AFTER LEAVING A meeting about preliminary marketing plans for a new educational program, Keleya returned to her office and checked her texts. *Leya what u been up to? Haven't talked to u in 2 days. Call me ASAP.* Keleya sat her cell phone down, picked up the office phone and called JaCola. "Hey Cola."

"Hey, how you feelin?"

"Girl, I'm alright," Keleya responded. "I'm kind of busy right now, so I'll have to call you later."

"Alright. I'll be home around 7:00."

"Okay." Before hanging up the phone, Keleya changed her mind. "Actually, why don't you and Maleek come over? I'll cook ya'll dinner."

"For real? You so sweet. We'll be there at 7:00."

"What do you want me to make?"

"I don't care. You decide."

"Alright then, I'll think of somethin."

When Keleya left work, she stopped by the grocery store to purchase a bag of red potatoes, four catfish filets, a loaf of white bread and a new bottle of ketchup. She went home and relaxed for a minute before cooking. Right after she placed a fresh pitcher of cherry Kool-Aid in the refrigerator, JaCola knocked on the door. She walked in with her son and removed his coat. After JaCola changed the channel to Nickelodeon and admonished Maleek to stay seated on the couch, she walked to the kitchen island and took a seat. "Girl that fish smells good. What else you makin?"

"Smothered potatoes," Keleya replied. "And I made you some cherry Kool-Aid."

JaCola smiled. After a few seconds, she asked, "So?"

"So what?"

"Why you always make me wait for information you know I want?"

"Cause I know you want it," Keleya laughed.

"I talked to my sister."

"Why?" Keleya asked as she turned to look at JaCola. She felt Angie's knowledge of the situation had no bearing upon Jordan's actions. "I asked you not to."

"Well I wanted to know if she knew what the hell was going on between them...she said she didn't know and if she had known she wouldn't have introduced ya'll." Keleya looked at JaCola again. "What?"

"That don't matter Cola. I understand that's your sister and you wanting to know if she would be triflin enough to keep the shit secret, but that doesn't change anything."

After considering what Keleya said, JaCola slid off the bar stool to check on Maleek. Because he continued to be still and quiet, she returned for more information from her best friend. "Has she called yet?"

Keleya turned the eye off and moved the grease filled cast iron skillet to the back of the stove. "She came over Wednesday after work." JaCola sat quietly with a questionable expression. "Don't look at me like that! Nothin happened."

JaCola cleared her face and asked, "What did she say?"

"Basically...she said she was sorry, but she wasn't sorry.

That she was wrong, but I deserved it."

"That you deserved it!"

"She didn't say it like that, but she might as well have... it's complicated cause I understand where she comin from, but she still wrong...and she mentioned the whole thing with Kris...she thinks I'm still in love with her."

"No, I don't think that's the case. If you felt that way about Kris, you wouldn't have been with Jordan in the first place...Leya."

"What?"

"Do you think you took things too fast or too far?"

Keleya exhaled, closing her eyes as she rubbed her forehead. "You sound like Zana...I don't know...maybe...but I tried to do things...right."

"Well...I told you before and I'm sayin it again. You and Kris got some unresolved shit to work out and now it's obvious...I know it's been a minute since ya'll talked, but you should call her," JaCola advised.

"I don't know. I'll think about it."

Keleya, JaCola and Maleek sat and ate at the dining room table. After they finished the meal and straightened the kitchen, Keleya and JaCola returned to the table and talked. "Do you still wanna be with Jordan?" JaCola asked. Keleya stared at the tabletop, spinning her cell phone repetitively. "You can tell me if you do."

"I liked what we had, but after she told me that she'd been sleepin with Renée for months, hell no! But I ain't gone lie and say it's easy to walk away...why you think I been havin such a fucked up year? I mean...there are good things and good times and I am livin...and I'm going to run this program...but what's up with the other shit?"

"I don't know Leya...you just need to put some things

into perspective and keep your priorities straight…that's the only thing we all can do."

After that comment, we talked about some other things. JaCola talked with me about her family—specifically her sister, Sonya, who has been estranged from their family for several years. Around 10:00, JaCola bundled her son tightly and they left. I was glad that she took me up on my offer to come over because I really needed someone to talk to and listen. I would have loved for that person to be Jordan, but that would never happen again.

December 28th

KELEYA CONSIDERED JACOLA'S suggestion for several days. She went back and forth with whether or not she would contact Kris. Eventually, she came to the conclusion that she had nothing to lose and that she wanted closure. While at work, she called Kris to ask if they could get together the next day. Kris agreed to meet and asked if Keleya would come to her place. Keleya thought it best to meet at a public and neutral location, but she reconsidered. She was interested in seeing Kris and Dréa's apartment.

• • •

When Keleya got home from work, she cooked an early dinner and talked to her mother for a while. After their conversation, she left for Kris' apartment. She called Kris to announce her arrival before getting out the car. As she walked up the stairs to the second floor apartment, Kris stepped outside onto the balcony. "Hey."

"What's up? Come in," Kris directed. Keleya walked past Kris and into a spotless apartment, recollecting that she was always tidy and clean. "Have a seat." Keleya sat on the couch and placed her purse next to her leg as Kris sat perpendicular to her on the love seat. "It's cold outside. Why don't you have on a coat?"

"I was just walkin upstairs," Keleya smiled. "I got on a long sleeved shirt."

Kris smiled and placed her cell phone on the coffee table. "How was your Christmas?"

"It was good. But it was a little different being with my family this year because last year I was with you in St. Louis." Keleya felt a little awkward after making that statement. She could tell that Kris felt similarly, so she immediately switched the topic. "What are your plans for New Year's?"

"I don't know. I haven't thought about it."

On the verge of Kris' next statement, Dréa walked into the living room. And by the look on her face, she was not forewarned of Keleya's visit. "What's up?" Dréa said with reservation.

"Hey Dréa."

Dréa walked to the front door. It seemed as if she wanted to say more, but she declined. "Ah cuz, let me talk to you for a second," she requested before stepping outside.

"I'll be right back." Less than thirty seconds later, Kris stepped into the apartment again and locked the door. When she was seated, Keleya asked how she'd been. "I been a'ight. Just tryin to make it day-by-day."

"What about Takira and Davian?" Keleya asked.

"They doing good. They ask about you all the time. You should call them."

"Yeah, I should...what about your girlfriend?"

Kris smiled and shook her head. "I don't have a girlfriend and you know that."

"Kris, I can build a house with the things I don't know... what? Is she out of the picture or do you call her somethin different?"

Kris laughed. "We kick it sometimes…but right now I need to be by myself. What about you?"

"We're not together anymore."

Kris seemed reluctant to ask the following question, but she asked anyway. "What happened?"

Keleya exhaled and crossed her arms. "I don't wanna get into that."

Kris moved to the edge of the love seat and looked at Keleya. "Leya…I'm sorry about what happened that night, you know, with the CD. I didn't want all that to go down."

Keleya didn't expect Kris to introduce past events into the conversation, but she was glad that she did. "What was the problem? Why didn't you want me to have it?"

"Honestly…I was with Soria and she was drinkin with some friends and gettin on my last nerve…one of her friends said somethin that reminded me of you…and I missed you. Dréa had already told me that she left the CD, so I used it as an excuse to see you. I don't know how Soria knew that I was over there…and I ain't gone lie, I was mad as hell when I realized you were in there with your girl…but like I said, I'm sorry."

"After it was all said and done, it wasn't that big of a deal," Keleya stated. After a few seconds, she continued. "Kris…I need to be upfront with you…I feel like we ended things, but we never came back to the table to talk about it or deal with it…at first I didn't want to, but I think about you sometimes…I think about what we had and what happened and I wonder was it worth it…I know some things changed at some point in our relationship…but umm…how do you feel?"

Kris stared at the floor for a moment. "I feel like you didn't give me the opportunity to make things right…we got into it and you walked out. That was it…then we started talkin again, we went out a few times and we…we had sex and we pushed each other away. Shit, I'm not a puppy Keleya. I moved on."

"But do you understand why I did that? I was hurt Kris. After I realized you were messin with Soria, that shit hurt even more…you didn't go find some new random chick. You went a block away. This was the same girl who'd been in our apartment before, so what was I supposed to think? That said to me that you wanted her all along and when you had the opportunity, you took it."

"I didn't have feelings for her. I never have. She was just there."

"Okay. She was convenient, but what about the other one? You obviously had feelings for her and you acted out on them. You met her one day, talked to her behind my back and had sex with her a week later."

Kris stared at the floor again before looking at Keleya with vast regret in her eyes. "Leya…I…yes I was texting her and I saw her that night you went to work and me and Dréa went out…but *nothing* happened. I didn't kiss her or even touch her. We didn't have sex."

Upon hearing those words, everything inside of Keleya shut down. She just stared at Kris, but Kris looked away fearful of what Keleya's reaction would be. Eventually, Keleya took a breath and her heart dropped as tears rolled down her face. She grabbed her purse and stood to immediately leave, but Kris stepped in her path before she reached the door. Kris barricaded the exit with her person and took hold of Keleya's arms. "Leya don't leave. I wanna talk to you about this."

"Let me go!"

"I'm not lettin you walk out."

Keleya snatched her body away and took a few steps back. After wiping tears, she looked at Kris and yelled, "Kriston, get the fuck out of my way!"

"No! I'm not movin!"

Keleya turned her back to Kris. She wondered if there was

another way out the apartment, but there wasn't. So she turned around to face Kris. "Why would you destroy what we had by lyin to me about sleepin with that girl?"

"I never told you that I slept with her."

"What?" Keleya asked as she instantly replayed scenes of that February night in her head. "You *let* me believe it." Keleya paused and shook her head. "All you had to do was tell me I was wrong Kris…I loved you!" At this point, Keleya was so overwhelmed with emotion that she returned to the couch and cried.

"If you wanna leave, go," Kris said as she stepped away from the door.

Keleya wiped her tears and looked at the wall. "No! Bring yo ass over here and sit down! I wanna know why you allowed a lie to keep us from being together."

Kris walked over and took a seat beside Keleya. "Leya… when we graduated, you didn't wanna come back here. We moved back because I wanted to…when we got here things were cool, but after a while, you started to resent me for being somewhere you didn't wanna be…there were days when I looked at you and could tell that you hated me for it. And the main way you showed me how you felt was by using sex as a way to control our relationship…so when that shit went down with Jazmine and you assumed that I slept with her, I held my tongue cause I felt like it would be your chance to leave…that's what you wanted anyway. You were just waitin for a reason to leave. And after we argued that night, you walked out and didn't come back. On one hand, I wanted that to happen, but at the same time, that shit pissed me the fuck off cause I wanted you to fight for me and you didn't! I thought the woman I loved would raise hell to be with me no matter what! So I said fuck it, you can believe whatever the hell you wanna believe."

"I never wanted to be in Memphis, but I wanted to be

wherever you were…I didn't need you to sacrifice our relationship to make me happy. As you see, at the end of the day, the shit didn't work! And regardless of where we stood at the time, I was willing to do *whatever* it took to be with you… we could have worked shit out!" Keleya wiped her face again and stared at the floor. She was emotionally drained and could take no more. She stood up and headed for the door, this time with no interference.

I really didn't have the strength to drive home, but I couldn't stay. So I sat in the car a couple of minutes to pull myself together. When I did get home, I went straight to bed and I cried myself to sleep.

January 17th

Kriston,

Last night while lying in the bed, I heard a song by Fantasia that brought tears to my eyes. I've heard "Bittersweet" several times before, but it wasn't until I listened to the lyrics again that I realized how much I identified with the song. There was something about that moment that allowed me to put multiple things into perspective.

I'm sending you this email because there are some things I need to get off my chest. Even though we're not together, you still affect me. I care about you and I can't let things that have come between us continue to weigh on my heart. You were my best friend and I valued our friendship. And despite everything, you're still special to me.

So first, let me say I'm sorry. I apologize for not trusting and supporting you enough to keep our relationship positive. I'm sorry for pressuring you about things you could not control. I'm sorry for pushing us from the center of our relationship. And I'm sorry that I let the fact that I was unhappy with some things in my life create a barrier between us. I wish we both had done some things differently, but neither one of us can turn back the hands of time. All I can do is take accountability for my actions and focus on the now and the future.

When I was thinking about writing you this letter, I thought about the first time that I knew beyond a shadow of doubt that I loved you. It was spring semester junior year when you came back from your semester abroad in Ghana. Of course I didn't want you to go, but we both knew that the opportunity and experience was worth leaving me for four months! When you got back, you came to my room and we held each other for hours, and then you told me that you'd brought me something. You left and came back five minutes later with this huge ass box. And when I opened it, I couldn't believe my eyes. You managed to ship back a piece of beautifully hand carved wood just for me, and you said the man who made the mask created it to glorify women. I took it out the box and rubbed my hands across the whole thing. You asked me if I liked it and I said that I loved it because it was the closest I'd ever been to Africa. I knew it was just an object, but it meant the world to me. It represented you coming back to me and being permanent in my life. And I never wanted you to leave again.

That's making me emotional so I'm moving on...I hope you and your family are well. And I hope you had a good New Year's. Maybe we can get together with the children again. They would enjoy it and I would too.

Before I end, I want to invite you to a reception that I'm having on the 31st for the launch of a mentorship program that I'm directing. There will be various community agencies there and hopefully local media will show up. This is something that is very important to me and I really want you to be there. I've attached a PDF of the official invite.

Always,

Keleya

After I sent the email I felt relieved. It took a while, but I was finally honest with myself about the fact that I wanted Kris in my life. But I didn't necessarily want us to be together. I just needed us to be friends again. She was such a big part of my support system in the past, and I felt my foundation weaken when our friendship dissolved...I just hope that she still feels that same way about me.

March 6th

I RECEIVED AN unexpected phone call from Jordan yesterday. She asked if I could meet her at the park today. Since I had an underlying desire to make amends, I agreed. When I arrived, we sat on the bench of our first date to talk. She asked me about the program and I told her it was going very well. I explained that I had fourteen participating teenagers paired with adults of diverse backgrounds and that I was in the process of applying for additional funding from other sources. "What about you? How are things going for you?"

"Good. Work is crazy, but I'm good. And...you were right. My grandmother pulled through. She's been a lot better," Jordan explained.

"That's good to hear...so what does that mean for you and your mother?"

"She actually left a few weeks ago...and I'm leaving at the end of the month. I'm finally leaving this damn city," Jordan smiled. Then she looked in my eyes. "That's why I called and asked you to meet me here...I've definitely had some regrets... and to be honest, I've missed you. But I'm not here to ask you for anything. I just wanted to say goodbye...so thanks for coming because I wanted to see you before I left. I didn't think this would be appropriate over the phone because...you deserve more than that."

"I was extremely surprised when you called, but I'm glad you did...I want you to know that despite the trials and errors, I can honestly say that I'm happier now. And regardless of what happened between us, I have you to thank for a big part of it...I've spent a lot of time reflecting on my actions and how they've affected other people...and no matter how long it took for it to happen, I'm glad that I had people in my life, like you, that would be honest with me...Jordan, you did something wonderful for me. You helped me find something that has made me content with a big part of my life...and I hope the best for you. I really do."

A few minutes later, we stood from the bench to leave. But before saying goodbye, I stepped closer to Jordan to gently touch her face and to give her a farewell kiss. As Jordan hugged me, I told her to take care of herself. After she said the same and let me go, I walked away.

I walked back to my car and opened the passenger side door. I got in and put on the seat belt. Kris stared at me for several seconds before starting the car. "Did you have to kiss her?" she asked.

I looked at Kris and smiled. "Let's go."